Eleanor Frances Poynter

My little lady

Eleanor Frances Poynter

My little lady

ISBN/EAN: 9783337111557

Printed in Europe, USA, Canada, Australia, Japan

Cover: Foto ©Andreas Hilbeck / pixelio.de

More available books at **www.hansebooks.com**

Thy sinless progress, through a world
By sorrow darken'd and by care disturb'd,
Apt likeness bears to hers through gather'd clouds
Moving untouch'd in silver purity.

WORDSWORTH.

IN THREE VOLUMES.

VOL. I.

LONDON:

HURST AND BLACKETT, PUBLISHERS,

13, GREAT MARLBOROUGH STREET.

1871.

The right of Translation is reserved.

LONDON:
PRINTED BY MACDONALD AND TUGWELL, BLENHEIM HOUSE,
BLENHEIM STREET, OXFORD STREET

TO

J. C. I.

MY LITTLE LADY.

PART I.

CHAPTER I.

IN THE GARDEN.

THERE are certain days in the lives of each one of us, which come in their due course without special warning, to which we look forward with no anticipations of peculiar joy or sorrow, from which beforehand we neither demand nor expect more than the ordinary portion of good and evil, and which yet through some occurrence—unconsidered perhaps at the moment, but gaining in significance with years and connecting events—are destined to live apart in our memories to the end of our existence. Such a day in Horace Graham's life was a certain hot Sunday in August, that he spent at the big hotel at Chaudfontaine.

Every traveller along the great high road leading from Brussels to Cologne knows Chaudfontaine, the little village distant about six miles from Liége, with its church, its big hotel, and its scattered cottages, partly forges, partly restaurants, which shine white against a dark green background of wooded hills, and gleam reflected in the clear tranquil stream by which they stand. On every side the hills seem to fold over and enclose the quiet green valley; the stream winds and turns, the long poplar-bordered road follows its course; amongst the hills are more valleys, more streams, woods, forests, sheltered nooks, tall grey limestone rocks, spaces of cornfields, and bright meadows. Everyone admires the charming scenery as the train speeds across it, through one tunnel after another; but there are few amongst our

countrymen who care to give it more than a
passing glance of admiration, or to tarry in
the quiet little village even for an hour, in
their great annual rush to Spa, or the Rhine,
or Switzerland. As a rule one seldom meets
Englishmen at Chaudfontaine, and it was
quite by chance that Horace Graham found
himself there. An accident to a goods train
had caused a detention of several hours all
along the line, as he was travelling to Brussels, and it was by the advice of a Belgian
fellow-passenger that he had stopped at
Chaudfontaine, instead of going on to Liége,
as he had at first proposed doing, on hearing
from the guard that it was the furthest point
that could be reached that night.

Behind the hotel lies a sunshiny shady
garden, with benches and tables set under
the trees near the house, and beyond, an unkempt lawn, a sort of wilderness of grass
and shrubs and trees, with clumps of dark

and light foliage against the more uniform green of the surrounding hills, and it was still cool and pleasant when Graham wandered into it after breakfast on that Sunday morning, whilst all in front of the hotel was already basking in the hot sunshine. He had gone to bed the night before with the fixed intention of leaving by the earliest morning train, for his first impressions of Chaudfontaine had not been cheerful ones. It was nearly midnight when, with his companions, he had crossed the bridge that connects the railway station with the hotel on the opposite side of the stream, and scarcely a light was shining from the windows of the dim white building before him; he was very tired, rather cross, and disposed to grumble at the delay in his journey; and the general aspect of things— the bad supper, the sleepy waiter carrying a candle up flights of broad shallow wooden stairs, and down a long passage to a remote room barely furnished, the uncertain view of a foreground of rustling poplars, and close behind them a black silent mass of hill—all these had not tended to encourage him.

But a man must be very cynical, or very *blasé*, or wholly possessed by some other uncomfortable quality, who does not feel much cheered and invigorated by morning sunbeams pouring into a strange bed-room, and awakening him to new scenes and unexperienced sensations. Horace Graham was neither cynical nor *blasé*; on the contrary, he was a pleasant-tempered, fresh-hearted lad of twenty or thereabouts, who only three weeks before had made his first acquaintance with French gendarmes, and for the first time had heard children shouting to each other in a foreign tongue along white-walled, sunshiny, foreign

streets.   Three weeks touring in Germany
had only served to arouse in him a passion
for travelling and seeing, for new places and
peoples and scenes, that in all his life, perhaps, would not be satiated; everything was
new to him, everything amused him; and
so it happened that, while he was dressing
and studying from his window the view that
had been only obscurely hinted at in the
darkness of the night before, a sudden desire
came over him to remain where he was for
that day, climb the hills that rose before
him, and see what manner of country lay
beyond.

It was still early when, after breakfasting
by himself in the salle-à-manger, he found
his way into the garden; no one was stirring,
it seemed deserted; he wandered along
the gravel paths, trod down the tall grass
as he crossed the lawn, and arrived at
the confines of the little domain. On two

sides it was bounded by a narrow stream, separating it from the road beyond; at the angle of the garden the shallow, trickling water widened into a little fall crossed by a few planks; there were trees and bushes on each side, and the grassy garden bank sloped down to the stream. It was very green, and peaceful and dewy. Horace stood still for a minute looking at the flickering lights and shadows, and watching the dash and current of the water.

"*Fi donc, Mademoiselle, tu n'es pas raisonnable,*" cries a sweet shrill little voice close to him, "*tu es vraiment insupportable aujourd'hui.*"

He turned round and saw a child between five and six years old, dressed in a shabby little merino frock and white pinafore, standing with her back towards him, and holding out a doll at arm's length, its turned-out pink leather toes just touching the ground.

" *Veux-tu bien être sage?*" continues the
small monitress with much severity, " *encore
une fois, un, deux, trois!* " and she made a
little dancing-step backwards ; then with an
air of encouragement, " *Allons, mon amie,
du courage!* We must be perfect in our
steps for this evening, for you know, Sophie,
if you refuse to dance, M. le Prince will be
in despair, and M. le Baron will put his hand
on his heart and cry, ' Alas, mademoiselle,
you have no pity, and my heart is deso-
lated !'"

" Madelon!" cries a voice through the trees
in the distance.

" *Me voici,* papa !" she answered, stopping
the dancing-lesson and looking round. As
she did so she caught sight of Horace, and
gazed up in his face with a child's deliberate
stare. She had great brown eyes, a little
round fair face, and light hair curling all
over her head. She looked up at him quite

fearlessly for a moment, and then darted away, dashing against somebody who was coming along the path, and disappeared.

"Take care, *ma petite*; you nearly knocked me down!" cried a good-humoured voice, belonging to a large gentleman with a ruddy face, and black hair and beard. "Ah! good morning, Monsieur," he continued as he approached Horace; "I rejoice to see that you have not yet quitted Chaudfontaine, as you spoke of doing last night."

"I have changed my mind," said Horace, smiling as he recognized his fellow-traveller of the night before. "I think of staying here to-day, and not leaving for Brussels till to-morrow morning."

"You will not regret it," said his companion, as they turned back towards the hotel, and walked on slowly together; "it is true there is not much here to tempt you during the day; but numbers will arrive

for the four o'clock *table-d'hôte*. In the
evening there will be quite a little society,
and we shall dance. I assure you, monsieur, that we also know how to be gay at
Chaudfontaine."

"I don't doubt it," answered Graham;
"and though I don't care much about
dancing——"

"You don't care about dancing?" interrupted the Belgian with astonishment; "but
that is of your nation, Monsieur. You are
truly an extraordinary people, you English;
you travel, you climb, you ride, you walk,
and you do not dance!"

"I think we dance too, sometimes," said
the young Englishman, laughing; "but I
own that it is walking I care for most just
now—the country about here seems to be
wonderfully pretty."

"In fact it is not bad," said the Belgian,
with the air of paying it a compliment;

" and if you take care to return in time for
the four o'clock *table-d'hôte*, you cannot do
better than make a little promenade to gain
an appetite for dinner. I can promise you
an excellent one—they keep an admirable
cook. I entreat of you not to think of
leaving for Brussels ; and precisely you cannot go," he added, drawing out his watch,
" for it is just the hour that the train leaves,
and I hear the whistle at this moment."

And, in fact, though they could not see
the train from where they stood, they heard
its shrill whistle as it rushed into the station
on the other side of the river.

" So it is decided," said Graham, " and I
remain."

" And you do wisely, Monsieur," cried
his companion ; " believe me, you will not
regret passing a day in this charming little
spot. Do they speak much in England of
Chaudfontaine, monsieur ?"

"Well, no," Horace was obliged to acknowledge, "they do not."

"Ah!" said the Belgian, a little disappointed; "but they speak of Brussels, perhaps?"

"Oh! yes, every one knows Brussels," answered Graham.

"It is a beautiful city," remarked his companion, "and has a brilliant society; but for my part, I own that at this season of the year I prefer the retirement, the tranquillity of Chaudfontaine, where also one amuses oneself perfectly well. I always spend two or three months here—in fact, have been here for six weeks already this summer. Affairs called me to Aix-la-Chapelle last week for a few days, and that was how I had the good fortune to meet Monsieur last night."

"It was very lucky for me," said Horace. "I am delighted to be here. The hotel

seems to be very empty," he added. " I
have seen nobody this morning except one
little girl."

" But no, the hotel is almost full—people
are gone to mass, perhaps, or are in bed, or
are breakfasting. It is still early."

"That little girl," said Horace—" does
she belong to the house ?"

" You mean the little girl who ran against
me as I came up to you just now ? No,
the *propriétaire* of the hotel has but one
daughter, Mademoiselle Cécile, a most
amiable person. But I know that child—
her father is one of the *habitués* of the
hotel. She is much to be pitied, poor little
one !"

" Why ?" asked Graham.

" Because her father—*ah ! bon jour, Madame*—excuse me, Monsieur, but I go to
pay my respects to Madame la Comtesse !"
cried the Belgian, as an elderly red-faced

lady, with fuzzy sandy hair, wearing a
dingy, many-flounced lilac barége gown,
came towards them along the gravel path.

"At last we see you back, my dear Monsieur!" she cried—"ah! how many regrets
your absence has caused!—of what an insupportable *ennui* have we not been the
victims!   But you are looking better than
when you left us; your journey has done
you good; it is plain that you have not suffered from absence."

"Alas! Madame," cries the other, "you
little know!   And how, for my part, can I
venture to believe in regrets that have left
no traces?   Madame is looking more charming, more blooming——"

Horace waited to hear no more; he left
the pair standing and complimenting each
other on the sunny pathway, and wandered
away under the shade of the big trees,
crossed the little stream and the white

dusty road beyond, and began to ascend the hills.

"What an ugly old woman!" thought the lad. "She and my friend seem to be great allies; she must be at least ten years older than he is, and he talks to her as if she were a pretty girl; but she is a Countess apparently, and I suppose that counts for something. Oh! what a jolly country!"

He strode along whistling, with his hands in his pockets, feeling as if he had the world before him to explore, and in the happiest of moods. Such a mood was not rare with Horace Graham in these youthful days, when, by force of good health and good spirits, and a large capacity for fresh genuine enjoyment, he was apt to find life pleasant enough on the whole, though for him it lacked several of the things that go to make up the ordinary ideal of human happiness. He was not rich; he had no

particular expectations, and but few family
ties, for his parents had both died when he
was very young, and except an aunt who
had brought him up, and a married sister
several years older than himself, he had no
near relations in the world. He was simply
a medical student, with nothing to look forward to but pushing his own way, and making his own path in life as best he could.
But he had plenty of talent, and worked
hard at his profession, to which he was devoted for reasons quite unconnected with
any considerations of possible profit and
loss.   Indeed, having just enough money
of his own to make him tolerably independent, he was wont to ignore all such
considerations in his grand youthful way,
and to look upon his profession from a
purely abstract scientific point of view.
And yet he was not without large hopes,
grand vague ambitions concerning his future

career; for he was at an age when it seems
so much easier to become one of the few
enumerated great ones of the world than to
remain amongst the nameless forgotten mul-
titudes; and life lay before him rather as
something definite, which he could take up
and fashion to his own pleasure, than as a
succession of days and years which would
inevitably mould and influence him in their
course. It is not wholly conceit, perhaps,
which so assures these clever lads of the
vastness of their untried capabilities, that
there are moments when they feel as if they
could grasp heaven and earth in their wide
consciousness; it is rather a want of experience and clearness of perception. Horace
Graham was not particularly conceited, and
yet, in common with many other men of
his age, he had a conviction that, in some
way or other, life had great exceptional
prizes in store for him; and indeed he was

so strong, and young, and honest-hearted, that he had been successful enough hitherto within his narrow limits. He had pleasant manners, too, and a pleasant face, which gained him as many friends as he ever cared to have; for he had a queer, reserved, unsociable twist in his character, which kept him aloof from much company, and rather spoilt his reputation for geniality and heartiness. He hated the hard work he had to go through in society ; so at least he was wont to grumble, and then would add, laughing, "I daresay I am a conceited puppy to say so ; but the fact is, there are not six people in the world whose company I would prefer to my own for a whole day."

He found his own company quite sufficient during all his wanderings through that long summer's day in the lovely country round Chaudfontaine, a country neither grand nor wild, hardly romantic, but with a charm of its own that enticed Graham onwards in spite of the hot August sun. It was so green, so peaceful, so out of the world; the little valleys were wrapped so closely amongst the hills, the streams came gushing out of the limestone rocks, dry water courses led him higher and higher up amongst the silent woods, which stretched away for miles on either hand. Sometimes he would come upon an open space, whence he could look down upon the broader valley beneath, with its quiet river flowing through the midst, reflecting white villages, forges, long rows of poplars, an occasional bridge, and here and there a long low island; or descending, he would find himself in some narrow ravine, cleft between grey rocky heights overgrown with brushwood and trailing plants, the road leading beside a marshy brook, full of rushes and forget-me-nots, and disappearing amongst the forest trees. All day long Graham wandered about that pleasant land, and it was long past the four o'clock dinner hour when he stood on the top of the hill he had seen that morning from his window, and looked across the wide view of woods and cornfields to where a distant cloud of smoke marked the city of Liége. Thence descending by a steep zig-zag path, with a bench at every angle, he crossed the road and the little rivulet, and found himself once more in the garden at the back of the hotel.

CHAPTER II.

IN THE SALON.

HE had left it in the morning dewy, silent, almost deserted ; he found it full of gaiety and life and movement, talking, laughing, and smoking going on, pretty bright dresses glancing amongst the trees, children swinging under the great branches, the flickering lights and shadows dancing on their white frocks and curly heads, white-capped bonnes dangling their *bébés*, papas drinking coffee and liqueurs at the little tables, mammas talking the latest Liége scandal, and discussing the newest Parisian

fashions. The table-d'hôte dinner was just
over, and everybody had come out to enjoy
the air, till it was time for the dancing to
begin.

The glass door leading into the passage
that ran through the house stood wide open ;
so did the great hall door at the other end ;
and Graham could see the courtyard full of
sunshine, the iron railing separating it from
the road, the river gleaming, the bridge and
railway station beyond, and then again the
background of hills. He passed through
the house, and went out into the courtyard.
Here were more people, more gay dresses,
gossip, cigars, and coffee ; more benches and
tables set in the scanty shade of the formal
round-topped trees that stood in square
green boxes round the paved quadrangle.
Outside in the road, a boy with a monkey
stood grinding a melancholy organ ; the sun
seemed setting to the pretty pathetic tune,

which mingled not inharmoniously with the hum of voices and sudden bursts of laughter; the children were jumping and dancing to their lengthening shadows, but with a measured glee, so as not to disturb too seriously the elaborate combination of starch and ribbon and shining plaits which composed their fête day toilettes. A small tottering thing of two years old, emulating its companions of larger growth, toppled over and fell lamenting at Graham's feet as he came out. He picked it up, and set it straight again, and then, to console it, found a *sou*, and showed it how to put it into the monkey's brown skinny hand, till the child screamed with delight instead of woe. The lad had a kind, loving heart, and was tender to all helpless appealing things, and more especially to little children.

He stood watching the pretty glowing scene for a few minutes, and then went in

to his solitary *réchauffé* dinner. Coming out
again half an hour or so later, he found
everything changed. The monkey boy and
his organ were gone, the sun had set, twilight and mists were gathering in the valley,
and the courtyard was deserted; but across
the grey dusk, light was streaming through
the muslin window curtains of the salon,
the noise of laughter, and voices, and music
came from within now, breaking the evening stillness; for everyone had gone indoors
to the salon, where the gas was lighted,
chairs and tables pushed out of the way,
and Mademoiselle Cécile, the fat good-
natured daughter of the *propriétaire*, already
seated at the piano. The hall outside fills
with grinning waiters and maids, who have
their share of the fun as they look in through
the open door. Round go the dancers, slid-
ing and twirling on the smooth polished

floor, and Mademoiselle Cécile's fingers fly indefatigably over the keys, as she sits nodding her head to the music, and smiling as each familiar face glides past her.

Horace, who, after lingering awhile in the courtyard, had come indoors like the rest of the world, stood apart at the further end of the room, sufficiently entertained with looking on at the scene, which had the charm of novelty to his English eyes, and commenting to himself on the appearance of the dancers.

"But you do wrong not to dance, dear Monsieur, I assure you," said his Belgian friend, coming up to him at the end of a polka, with the elderly Countess, who with her dingy lilac barége gown exchanged for a dingier lilac silk, and her sandy hair fuzzier than ever, had been dancing vigorously. "Mademoiselle Cécile's music is delicious," he continued, "it positively inspires one; let me persuade you to attempt just one little dance."

"Indeed, I would rather look on," said Horace; "I can listen to Mademoiselle Cécile's music all the same, and I do not care much for dancing, as I told you; besides, I don't know anyone here."

"If that be all," cried the other eagerly, "I can introduce you to half a dozen partners in a moment; that lady that I have just been dancing with, for instance, will be charmed——"

"Stop, I entreat of you," said the young Englishman, in alarm, as his friend was about to rush off; "I cannot indeed—I assure you I am a very bad dancer; I am tired with my long walk too."

"Ah, that walk," said the Belgian, "I did wrong in advising you to take it; you prolonged it till you missed the *table d'hôte* din-

ner, and now you are too much fatigued
to dance."

" But I am very much amused as it is, I
assure you," insisted Graham. " Do tell me
something about all these people. Are
they all stopping at the hotel?"

His companion was delighted to give any
information in his power. No, not a third of
the people were stopping at the hotel, the
greater part had come over from Liége, and
would go back there by the ten o'clock
train.

" Then you do not know many of them?"
Graham said.

" No," the Belgian admitted, " he did not
know many of them; only those who were
staying at Chaudfontaine. That lady he had
just been dancing with, Monsieur had seen
in the morning, he believed; she was the
Countess G——, a most distinguished person,
with blood-royal in her veins, and came

from Brussels. That pretty girl in blue was
Mademoiselle Sophie L——, who was going to be married next month to one of the
largest proprietors in the neighbourhood,
the young man standing by her, who was
paying her so much attention. The odd-
looking man in shoes and buckles was a
rising genius, or thought himself so, a violinist, who came over occasionally from
Liége, and hoped to make his fortune some
day in London or Paris; and perhaps he
will do so," says the Belgian, "for he has
talent. That little dirty-looking young man
with a hooked nose, and the red Turkish
slippers, is a Spaniard going through a course
of studies at Liége; he is staying in the hotel,
and so are the fat old gentleman and lady
seated on the sofa; they are Brazilians, and
he has been sent over by his Government to
purchase arms, I believe. Those three young
ladies in white are sisters, and are come

here from Antwerp for the summer; that is
their mother talking to Mademoiselle Cécile. I see no one else at this moment," he
added, looking slowly round the room at the
groups of dancers who stood chattering and
fanning themselves in the interval between
the dances.

"Who is that?" asked Graham, directing
his attention to a gentleman who had just
appeared, and was standing, leaning in the
doorway opposite.

He was a tall handsome man, with light
hair, and a long fair moustache and beard,
perfectly well dressed, and with an air sufficiently distinguished to make him at once
conspicuous amongst the Liége clerks and
shopkeepers, of whom a large part of the
company consisted.

"Ah! precisely, Monsieur, you have fixed
upon the most remarkable personage here,"
cried his companion, with some excite-

ment; "but is it possible you do not know him?"

"I never saw him before," answered Graham. "Is he a celebrity? A prince, or an ambassador, or anything of that kind?"

"No, nothing of that kind," said the other laughing, "but a celebrity nevertheless in his way. That is M. Linders, the great gambler."

"I never even heard of him," said the young Englishman; "but then I don't know much about such people."

"It is true, I had forgotten that Monsieur is not of this country; but you would hear enough about him were you to stay any time at Wiesbaden, or Homburg, or Spa, or any of those places. He twice broke the bank at Homburg last year, won two hundred thousand francs at Spa this summer, and lost them again the next week. He is a most dangerous fellow, and positively dreaded by the proprietors of the tables."

"What! when he loses two hundred thousand francs?"

"Ah! that is a thing that rarely happens; as a rule he is perfectly cool, which is the principal thing at these tables, plays when the run is in his favour, and stops when it is against him; but occasionally he gets excited, and then of course the chances are that he loses everything like another."

"What can he be doing here?" said Graham.

"Who knows? Stopping a night or two on his way to Paris, or Brussels, perhaps, on the chance of finding some one here rich enough and imprudent enough to make it worth his while. You do not play, Monsieur?"

"Never in that way," answered the lad,

laughing; " I can get through a game of whist decently enough, but I rarely touch cards at all."

"Ah, then you are safe : otherwise I would have said, avoid M. Linders ; he has not the best reputation in the world, and he has a brother-in-law who generally travels with him, and is even a greater rogue than himself, but not so lucky—so they say at least."

" Do you know him, this famous gambler ? He does not look much like one," said Graham.

"That is true ; but he is a man of good birth and education, I believe, though he has turned out such a *mauvais sujet*, and it is part of his *métier* to get himself up in that style. Yes, I know him a little, from meeting him here and elsewhere ; he is al-ways going about, sometimes *en prince*, sometimes in a more humble way—but excuse me, dear Monsieur, Mademoiselle Cécile has begun to play, and I am engaged to Mademoiselle Sophie for this dance; she will never forgive me if I make her wait."

The dancers whirled on; the room grew hotter and hotter. M. Linders had disappeared, and Graham began to think that he too had had almost enough of it all, and that it would be pleasant to seek peace and coolness in the deserted moonlit courtyard. He was watching for a pause in the waltz, that would admit of his crossing the room, when his attention was attracted by the same little girl he had seen that morning in the garden. She was still dressed in the shabby old frock and pinafore, and as she came creeping in, threading her way deftly amongst the young ladies in starched muslins and gay ribbons who were fluttering about, she made the effect of a little brown

moth who had strayed into the midst of
a swarm of brilliant butterflies. No one
took any notice of her, and she made her
way up to the large round table which had
been pushed into the far corner of the room,
and near which Graham was standing.

"Do you want anything?" he asked, as
he saw her raise herself on tiptoe, and
stretch forward over the table.

"I want *that*," she said, pointing to a
miniature roulette board, which stood in
the middle, beyond the reach of her small
arm.

He gave it to her, and then stood watching to see what she would do with it. She
set to work with great deliberation; first
pulling a handful of sugar-plums out of her
pocket, and arranging them in a little heap
at her side on the table, and then proceed-
ing with much gravity to stake them on
the numbers. She would put down a

bonbon and give the board a twirl; "*vingt-cinq*," she would say; the ball flew round and fell into a number; it might be ten, or twenty, or twenty-five, it did not much matter; she looked to see what it was, but right or wrong, never failed to eat the bonbon—an illogical result, which contrasted quaintly with the intense seriousness with which she made her stakes. Sometimes she would place two or three sugar-plums on one number, always naming it aloud— "*trente-et-un*," "*douze-premier*," "*douze-après*." It was the oddest game for a small thing not six years old; and there was something odd, too, in her matter-of-fact, business-like air, which amused Graham. He had seen gambling-tables during his three weeks' visit to Germany, and he felt sure that this child must have seen them too.

" Eh, what an insupportable heat !" cried a harsh high-pitched voice behind them.

" Monsieur Jules, I will repose myself for a
few minutes, if you will have the goodness
to fetch me a glass of *eau sucrée.* *Je n'en
peux plus!*"

Graham, recognizing the voice, turned
round, and saw the Countess G—— leaning
on the arm of a young man with whom she
had been dancing.

" But it is really stifling !" she exclaimed,
dropping into an arm-chair by the table as
her partner retired. "Monsieur does not
dance, apparently," she continued, addressing Horace. " Well, you are perhaps right ;
it is a delightful amusement, but on a night
like this——Ah ! here is little Madelon. I
have not seen you before to-day. How is it
you are not dancing?"

" I don't want to," answered the child,
giving the roulette-board a twirl.

" But that is not at all a pretty game that
you have there," said the Countess, shaking

her head; "it was not for little girls that Mademoiselle Cécile placed the roulette-board there. Where is your doll? why are you not playing with her?"

"My doll is in bed; and I like this best," answered the child indifferently. "*Encore ce malheureux trente-six! Je n'ai pas de chance ce soir!*"

"But little girls should not like what is naughty; and I think it would be much better if you were in bed too. Come, give me that ugly toy; there is Monsieur quite shocked to see you playing with it."

Madelon looked up into Horace's face with her wide-open gaze, as if to verify this wonderful assertion; and apparently satisfied that it had been made for the sake of effect, continued her game without making any reply.

"Oh, then, I really must take it away," said the Countess; "*allons*, be reasonable, *ma petite*; let me have that, and go and dance with the other little boys and girls."

" But I don't want to dance, and I like to play at this," cries Madelon with her shrill little voice, clutching the board with both her small hands, as the Countess tried to get possession of it ; " you have no right to take it away. Papa lets me play with it ; and I don't care for you ! Give it me back again, I say ; *je le veux, je le veux* !"

" No, no," answered the Countess, pushing it beyond Madelon's reach to the other side of the table. " I daresay you have seen your papa play at that game ; but children must not always do the same as their papas. Now, be good, and eat your bonbons like a sensible child."

" I will not eat them if I may not play for them !" cried the child ; and with one sweep of her hand she sent them all off the table on to the floor, and stamped on them again and again with her tiny foot. "You have no right to speak to me so!" she went on energetically; "no one but my papa speaks to me; and I don't know you, and I don't like you, and you are very ugly!" and then she turned her back on the Countess and stood in dignified silence.

"*Mais c'est un petit diable!*" cried the astonished lady, fanning herself vigorously with her pocket-handkerchief. She was discomfited though she had won the victory, and hailed the return of her partner with the *eau sucrée* as a relief. "A thousand thanks, M. Jules! What if we take another turn, though this room really is of an insufferable heat."

Madelon was left confronting Horace, a most ill-used little girl, not crying, but with flushed cheeks and pouting lips—a little girl who had lost her game and her bonbons, and felt at war with all the world in conse-

quence.   Horace was sorry for her; he,
too, thought she had been ill-used, and no
sooner was the Countess fairly off than he
said, very immorally, no doubt,

" Would you like to have your game back
again ?"

" No," said Madelon, in whom this speech
roused a fresh sense of injury ; " I have no
more bonbons."

Graham had none to offer her, and a
silence ensued, during which she stood leaning against the table, slowly scraping one
foot backwards and forwards over the remains of the scattered bonbons.   At last he
bethought him of a small bunch of charms
that he had got somewhere, and hung to his
watch-chain, and with which he had often
enticed and won the hearts of children.

" Would you like to come and look at
these ?" he said, holding them up.

"No," she replied, ungraciously, and retreating a step backwards.

"Not at this?" he said. "Here is a little steam engine that runs on wheels; and, see, here is a fan that will open and shut."

"No," she said again, with a determined little shake of her head, and still retreating.

"But only look at this," he said, selecting a little flexible enamel fish, and trying to lure back this small wild bird. "See this little gold and green fish, it moves its head and tail."

"No," she said once more, but the fish was evidently a temptation, and she paused irresolute for a moment; but Graham made a step forward, and this decided her.

"I don't care for *breloques*," she said, with disdain, "and I don't want to see them, I tell you." And then, turning round, she marched straight out of the room.

At that moment the music stopped, the waltzing ceased, and a line of retreat was left open for Graham.   He saw the Countess once more approaching, and availed himself of it; out of the noise and heat and crowd he fled, into the fresh open air of the quiet courtyard.

CHAPTER III.

IN THE COURTYARD.

THREE gentlemen with cigars, sitting on the bench under the salon windows, two more pacing up and down in the moonlight before the hall-door, and a sixth apparently asleep in a shadowy corner, were the only occupants of the courtyard. Graham passed them by, and sought solitude at the lower end, where he found a seat on the stone coping of the iron railing. The peace and coolness and silence were refreshing, after the heat and clamour of the salon: the broad harvest-moon had risen above the opposite ridge of hills, and flooded everything with clear light, the river gleamed and sparkled, the poplars threw long still shadows across the white road; now and then the leaves rustled faintly, some far-off voice echoed back from the hills, and presently from the hotel the sound of the music, and the measured beat of feet, came softened to the ear, mingled with the low rush of the stream, and the ceaseless ringing of the hammers in the village forges.

Horace had not sat there above ten minutes, and was debating whether—his Belgian friend notwithstanding—a stroll along the river-bank would not be a pleasanter termination to his evening than a return to the dancing, when he saw a small figure appear in the hall doorway, stand a moment as if irresolute, and then come slowly across the courtyard towards him. As she came near he recognized little Madelon. She paused

when she was within a yard or two of him,
and stood contemplating him with her hands
clasped behind her back.

"So you have come out too," he said.

"*Mais oui—tout ce tapage m'agace les
nerfs*," answered the child, pushing her hair
off her forehead with one of her old-fashioned
little gestures, and then standing motionless
as before, her hands behind her, and her
eyes fixed on Graham. Somehow he felt
strangely attracted by this odd little child,
with her quaint vehement ways and speeches,
who stood gazing at him with a look half
farouche, half confiding, in her great brown
eyes.

"Monsieur," she began, at last.

"Well," said Graham.

"Monsieur, I *would* like to see the little
green fish. May I look at it?"

"To be sure," he answered. "Come here,
and I will show it to you."

" And, Monsieur, I do like *breloques* very much," continues Madelon, feeling that this is a moment for confession.

" Very well, then, you can look at all these. See, here is the little fish to begin with."

" And may I have it in my own hand to look at ?" she asked, willing to come to some terms before capitulating.

" Yes, you shall have it to hold in your own hand, if you will come here."

She came close to him then, unclasping her hands, and holding out a tiny palm to receive the little trinket.

Horace was engaged in unfastening it from the rest of the bunch, and whilst doing so he said,

" Will you not tell me your name ? Madelon, is it not ?"

" My name is Madeleine, but papa and every one call me Madelon."

" Madeleine what ?"

" Madeleine Linders."

" Linders !" cried Horace, suddenly en-
lightened ; " what, is M. Linders—" the famous gambler he had nearly said, but checked
himself—" is that tall gentleman with a
beard, whom I saw in the salon just now,
your papa ? "

" Yes, that is my papa. Please may I
have that now ?"

He put the little flexible toy into her
hand, and she stood gazing at it for a moment, almost afraid to touch it, and then
pushing it gently backwards and forwards
with one finger.

" It does move !" she cried delighted. " I
never saw one like it before."

" Would you like to keep it ?" asked
Graham.

" Always, do you mean?—for my very
own ?"

"Yes, always."

"Ah, yes!" she cried, "I should like it very much. I will wear it round my neck with a string, and love it so much,—better than Sophie."

She looked at it with great admiration as it glittered in the moonlight; but her next question fairly took Horace aback.

"Is it worth a great deal of money, Monsieur?" she inquired.

"Why, no, not a great deal—very little, in fact," he replied.

"Ah! then, I will beg papa to let me keep it always, always, and not to take it away."

"I daresay he will let you keep it, if you tell him you like it," said Graham, not clearly understanding her meaning.

"Oh! yes, but then he often gives me pretty things, and then sometimes he says he must take them away again, because they are worth so much money. I don't mind, you know, if he wants them; but I will ask him to let me keep this."

"And what becomes of all your pretty things?"

"I don't know; I have none now," she answered, "we left them behind at Spa. Do you know one reason why I would not dance to-night?" she added, lowering her voice confidentially.

"No; what was it?"

"Because I had not my blue silk frock with lace, that I wear at the balls at Wiesbaden and Spa. I can dance, you know, papa taught me; but not in this old frock, and I left my other at Spa."

"And what were your other reasons?" asked Graham, wondering more and more at the small specimen of humanity before him.

"Oh! because the room here is so small
and crowded. At Wiesbaden there are rooms
large—so large—quite like this courtyard,"
extending her small arms by way of giving
expression to her vague sense of grandeur;
"and looking-glasses all round, and crimson
sofas, and gold chandeliers, and ladies in
such beautiful dresses, and officers who
danced with me. I don't know any one
here."

"And who were the Count and the Prince
you were talking about to Mademoiselle
Sophie in the garden this morning?"

Madelon looked disconcerted.

"I shan't tell you," she said, hanging
down her head.

"Will you not? Not if I want to know
very much?"

She hesitated a moment, and then burst
forth—

"Well, then, they were just nobody at

all. I was only talking make-believe to
Sophie, that she might do the steps properly."

"Oh! then, you did not expect to see
them here this evening?"

"Here!" cries Madelon, with much contempt; "why, no. One meets nothing but
bourgeois here."

Graham was infinitely amused.

"Am I *bourgeois?*" he said, laughing.

"I don't know," she replied, looking at
him; "but you are not a milord, I know,
for I heard papa asking Mademoiselle Cécile
about you, and she said you were not a
milord at all."

"So you care for nothing but Counts and
Princes?"

"I don't know," she said again. Then
with an evident sense that such abstract
propositions would involve her beyond her

depth, she added, " Have you any other pretty things to show me ? I should like to see what else you have on your chain."

In five minutes more they were fast friends, and Madelon, seated on Graham's knee, was chattering away, and recounting to him all the history of her short life. He was not long in perceiving that her father was the beginning and end of all her ideas —her one standard of perfection, the one medium through which, small as she was, she was learning to look out on and esti-mate the world, and receiving her first im-pressions of life. She had no mother, she said, in answer to Graham's inquiries. *Maman* had died when she was quite a little baby; and though she seemed to have some dim faint recollection of having once lived in a cottage in the country, with a woman

to take care of her, everything else referred to her father, from her first, vague
floating memories to the time when she
could date them as distinct and well-defined
facts. She had once had a nurse, she said
—a long time ago that was, when she was
little—but papa did not like her, and so
she went away; and now she was too big
for one. Papa did everything for her, it
appeared, from putting her to sleep at
night, when Mademoiselle was disposed to
be wakeful, to nursing her when she was
ill, taking her to fêtes on grand holidays,
buying her pretty things, walking with her,
teaching her dancing, and singing, and
reading; and she loved him so much—ah!
so much! Indeed, in all the world, the
child had but one object for a child's boundless powers of trust and love and veneration,
and that one was her father.

"And where do you generally live now?"
asked Graham.

"Why, nowhere in particular," Madelon
answered. "Of course not—they were
always travelling about. Papa had to go to
a great many places. They had come last
from Spa, and before that they had been at
Wiesbaden and Homburg, and last winter
they had spent at Nice; and now they were
on their way to Paris."

"And do you and your papa always live
alone? Have you not an uncle?" enquired
Graham, remembering the Belgian's speech
about the brother-in-law.

"Oh! yes, there is Uncle Charles—he
comes with us generally; but sometimes he
goes away, and then I am so glad."

"How is that? are you not fond of him?"

"No," said Madelon, "I don't like him
at all; he is very disagreeable, and teases
me. And he is always wanting me to go

away; he says, 'Adolphe'—that is papa, you
know—'when is that child going to school?'
But papa pays no attention to him, for he is
never going to send me away; he told me so,
and he says he could not get on without me
at all."

Graham no longer wondered at Madelon's
choice of a game, for it appeared she was in
the habit of accompanying her father every
evening to the gambling tables, when they
were at any of the watering-places he fre-
quented.

"Sometimes we go away into the ball-
room and dance," she said, "that is when
papa is losing; he says, 'Madelon, *mon
enfant*, I see we shall do nothing here to-
night, let us go and dance.' But sometimes
he does nothing but win, and then we stop
till the table closes, and he makes a great
deal of money. Do you ever make money
in that way, Monsieur?" she added naïvely.

"Indeed I do not," replied Graham.

"It is true that everyone has not the same way," said the child, with an air of being well informed, and evidently regarding her father's way as a profession like another, only superior to most. "What do you do, Monsieur?"

"I am going to be a doctor, Madelon."

"A doctor," she said reflecting; "I do not think that can be a good way. I only know one doctor, who cured me when I was ill last winter; but I know a great many gentlemen who make money like papa. Can you make a fortune with ten francs, Monsieur?"

"I don't think I ever tried," answered Horace.

"Ah well, papa can; I have often heard him say, 'Give me only ten francs, *et je ferai fortune!*'"

There was something at once so droll

and so sad about this child, with her precocious knowledge and ignorant simplicity,
that the lad's honest tender heart was
touched with a sudden pity as he listened
to her artless chatter. He was almost glad
when her confidences drifted away to more
childlike subjects of interest, and she told
him about her toys, and books, and pictures,
and songs; she could sing a great many
songs, she said, but Horace could not persuade her to let him hear one.

"Why do you talk French?" she said
presently; "you speak it so funnily. I can
talk English."

"Can you?" said Horace laughing, for
indeed he spoke French with a fine English accent and idiom. "Let me hear you.
Where did you learn it?"

"Uncle Charles taught me; he is English," she answered, speaking correctly
enough, with a pretty little accent.

" Indeed!" cried Graham. "Your mother was English, then ?"

" Yes. Mamma came from England, papa says, and Uncle Charles almost always talks English to me. I would not let him do it, only papa wished me to learn."

"And have you any other relations in England ?"

" I don't know," she answered. " We have never been in England, and papa says he will never go, for he detests the English; but I only know Uncle Charles and you, and I like you."

"What is your Uncle Charles' other name? Can you tell me ?"

" Leroy," she answered promptly.

" But that is not an English name," said Graham.

This was a little beyond Madelon, but after some consideration, she said with much simplicity,

" I don't know whether it is not English.
But it is only lately his name has been
Leroy, since he came back from a journey
he made; before that it was something else,
I forget what, but I heard him tell papa he
would like to be called Leroy, as it was a
common name; and papa told me, in case
anyone asked me."

" I understand," said Graham; and indeed
he did understand, and felt a growing compassion for the poor little girl, whose only
companions and protectors were a gambler
and a sharper.

They were still talking, when the silence
of the courtyard was broken by a sudden
confusion and bustle. The sound of the
music and dancing had already ceased; and
now a medley of voices, a shrill clamour of
talking and calling, made themselves heard
through the open hall door.

" Henri ! Henri ! ou est-il donc, ce petit
drôle?"

" Allons, Pauline, dépêche toi, mon enfant,
ton père nous attends !"

" Ciel! j'ai perdu mon fichu et mes gants."

" Enfin."

" The people are going away," says
Madelon ; and, in fact, in another minute
the whole party, talking, laughing, hurry-
ing, came streaming out by twos and
threes into the moonlight, and, crossing the
road and bridge, disappeared one by one in
the station beyond, the sound of their voices
still echoing back through the quiet night.
The last had hardly vanished when a tall
solitary figure appeared in the courtyard,
and advanced, looking round as if searching
for some one.

" Madelon !" cried the same voice that
Graham had heard that morning in the
garden.

"There is papa looking for me; I must go," exclaimed the child at the same moment; and before Graham had time to speak, she had slipped off his knee and darted up to her father; then taking his hand, the two went off together, the small figure jumping and dancing by the side of the tall man as they disappeared within the doorway of the hotel.

A few minutes more, and then a sound as of distant thunder told that the train was approaching through the tunnel. Graham watched it emerge, traverse the clear moonlit valley with slackening speed, and pause at the station for its freight of passengers. There was a vague sound of confusion as the people took their places, and then with a parting shriek it set off again; and as the sound died away in the distance, a great stillness succeeded the noise and bustle of a few moments before.

Horace was afraid he had seen the last of
Madelon, for returning to the hotel he
found no one in the salon, with the exception of Mademoiselle Cécile, who was already
putting out the lights. The hall, too, was deserted; the servants had vanished, and the
habitués of the hotel had apparently gone
to bed, for he met no one as he passed
along, and turned down the passage leading
to the salle-à-manger. This was a large long
room, occupying the whole ground floor of
one wing of the hotel, with windows looking out on one side into the courtyard, on
the other into the garden, two long tables,
smaller ones in the space between, and above
them a row of chandeliers smothered in pink
and yellow paper roses. The room looked
bare and deserted enough now; a sleepy
waiter lounged at the further end, the trees
in the garden rustled and waved to and fro
in the rising night breeze, the moonlight

streamed through the uncurtained windows on to the boarded floor and white table-cloths, chasing the darkness into remote corners, and contending with the light of the single lamp which stood on one of the smaller tables, where two men were sitting, drinking, smoking, and playing at cards.

One of them was a man between thirty and forty, in a tight fitting black coat buttoned up to his chin, and with a thin face, smooth shaven, with the exception of a little yellow moustache, and sharp grey eyes. He would have been handsome, had it not been for his unpleasant expression, at once knowing and suspicious. The other Horace immediately recognised as Monsieur Linders; and a moment afterwards he perceived little Madeleine, sitting nestled close up to her father's side. The lamplight shone on her curly head and innocent *mignonne* face as she watched the game with eager eyes; it

was piquet, and she was marking for her
father, and when he had a higher score than
his opponent, she laughed and clapped her
hands with delight.

Graham stood watching this little scene
for a minute; and somehow, as he looked at
the little motherless girl, there came the
thought of small rosy children he knew
far away in England, who, having said their
prayers, and repeated their Sunday hymns,
perhaps, had been tucked into little white
beds, and been fast asleep hours ago; and
a kind, foolish notion entered the young
fellow's head, that, for that one evening at
least, he must get the brown-eyed child,
who had taken his fancy so much, away
from the drinking, and smoking, and card-
playing, into a purer atmosphere. He went
up to the table, and leant over her chair.

"Will you come out again and have a walk
with me in the garden?" he said in English.

The man opposite, who was dealing, looked up sharply and suspiciously. Madelon turned round, and gazed up into the kind face smiling down on her, then shook her head with great decision.

" Not a little walk ?   I will tell you such pretty stories, all about fairies, and moonlight, and little boys and girls, and dragons," said Horace, drawing largely on his imagination, in his desire to offer a sufficient inducement.

"No," said Madelon, " I can't come ; I am marking for papa."

" What is it ?" said M. Linders, who understood very little English ; " what does this gentleman want, *mon enfant ?*"

" I was asking your little girl if she would take a walk with me in the garden," says Horace, getting rather red, and in his bad French.

"Monsieur is too good," answers M. Linders, making a grand bow, whilst his companion, having finished dealing, sat puffing away at his cigar, and drumming impatiently with his fingers on the table; "but the hour is rather late; what do you say, Madelon? Will you go with Monsieur?"

"No, papa," says the child, "I am marking for you; I don't want to go away."

"You see how it is, Monsieur," said M. Linders, turning to Graham with a smile and a shrug. "This little one thinks herself of so much importance, that she will not leave me."

"Are you then mad," cried his companion, "that you think of letting Madelon go out at this time of night? It is nearly eleven o'clock, and she can hardly keep her eyes open."

"My eyes are wide, wide open, Uncle Charles," exclaimed Madelon, indignantly;

" I'm not a bit tired, but I don't want to go out now."

" Monsieur will perhaps join our party," said Monsieur Linders, very politely. " I should be delighted to try my luck with a fresh adversary."

"Thank you," said Graham, "but I hardly ever touch cards." Then turning to Madelon, he added, " I must go away now, since you will not come for a walk. Won't you wish me good-bye? 1 shall not be here to-morrow."

She turned round and put her little hand into his for a moment; then with a sudden shy caprice snatched it away, and hid her face on her father's shoulder, just peeping at him with her bright eyes. But she started up again suddenly as he was leaving the room, calling out, "*Adieu, Monsieur, bon voyage,*" and kissing her hand to him. He smiled and nodded in return, bowed to M.

Linders, and so went away. There was a moment's silence after he went, and then, "You have made a fine acquaintance this evening, Madelon," said her uncle.

Madelon made a little *moue*, but did not answer.

"Are you then mad, Adolphe," he said again, "that you permit Madeleine to pick up an acquaintance with anyone who chooses to speak to her? An Englishman too!"

"Papa is not mad," cried Madelon, between whom and her uncle there was apparently a standing skirmish. "He was a very kind gentleman, and I like him very much; he gave me this little goldfish, and I shall keep it always, always," and she kissed it with effusion.

"Bah!" said M. Linders, "English or French, it is all one to me; and what harm could he do to the little one? It was an accident, but it does not matter for once.

Come, Madelon, you have forgotten to mark."

"It is your turn to deal next, papa," said the child, " may I do it for you ?"

Horace Graham left Chaudfontaine by the earliest train the following morning; and of all the people he had seen on that Sunday evening at the hotel, only two ever crossed his path again in after years—M. Linders, and his little daughter, Madeleine.

CHAPTER IV.

RETROSPECT.

M. LINDERS was of both Belgian and French extraction, his father having been a native of Liége, his mother a Parisian of good family, who, in a moment of misplaced sentiment, as she was wont in after years to sigh, had consented to marry a handsome young Belgian officer, and had expiated her folly by spending the greater part of her married life at Malines, where her husband was stationed, and at Liége, where his mother and sister resided. Adolphe's education, however, was wholly

French; for Madame Linders, who, during her husband's life, had not ceased to mourn over her exile from her own city, lost no time, after his death, in returning to Paris with her two children, Thérèse, a girl of about twelve, and Adolphe, then a child five or six years old.

Madame Linders had money, but not much, and she made it go further than did ever Frenchwoman before, which is saying a great deal. Adolphe must be educated, Adolphe must be clothed, Adolphe was to be a great man some day; he was to go into the army, make himself a name, become a General, a Marshal,—heaven knows what glories the mother did not dream for him, as she turned and twisted her old black silks, in the *entresol* in the Chaussée d'Antin, where she had her little apartment. She had friends in Paris, and must keep up appearances for Adolphe's sake, not to mention her own, and so could not possibly live in a cheap out-of-the-way quarter.

As for Thérèse, she was of infinitely small account in the family. She was plain, not too amiable, nor particularly clever, and inclined to be *dévote*; and, as in spite of positive and negative failings, she also had to eat and be clothed as well as her handsome fair brother, she could be regarded as nothing else than a burden in the economical household.

"You ask me what I shall do with Thérèse?" said Madame Linders one day to a confidential friend. "Oh! she will go into a convent, of course. I know of an excellent one near Liége, of which her aunt is the superior, and where she will be perfectly happy. She has a turn that way. What else can I do with her, my dear? To speak frankly, she is *laide à faire peur*, and she can have no *dot* worth mentioning, for

I have not a sou to spare; so there is no chance of her marrying."

Thérèse knew her fate, and was resigned to it. As her mother said, she had a turn that way; and to the Liége convent she according went, but not before Madame Linders' death, which took place when her daughter was about seven-and-twenty, and which was, as Thérèse vehemently averred, occasioned by grief at her son's conduct.

Adolphe had also known the fate reserved for him, and was by no means resigned to it; for he had never had the least intention of becoming a soldier, and having escaped conscription, absolutely refused to enter the army. He was a clever, unprincipled lad, who had done well at his studies, but lost no time in getting into the most dissipated society he could find from the moment he left college. He inherited his father's good looks, but his mother's predilections apparently; for he he set out in life with the determination to be Parisian amongst Parisians—of a certain class, be it understood ; and having some talent for drawing, as indeed he had for most things, he used it as a pretext, announced that he intended to be an artist, and furnishing a room in the Quartier Latin, with an easel and a pipe, he began the wild Bohemian life which he found most in accordance with his tastes.

He was selfish and reckless enough, but not altogether heartless, for he had a real affection for his mother, which might have been worked upon with advantage. But Madame Linders, who had indulged him till he had learnt to look upon her devotion as a thing of course, now turned upon him with the fretful, inconsequent reproaches of a weak mind ; and finding that he was constantly met with tearful words and aggrieved looks, her son avoided her as much as possible. His sister he could not endure. Thérèse had always been jealous of the marked preference shown for him ; and now, with an evident sense of triumph, she preached little sermons, talked at him with unceasing perseverance, and in truth was not a very engaging person.

Madame Linders had not been dead ten days, when the brother and sister had a violent quarrel, and parted with the determination on either side never to meet again—a resolution which was perfectly well kept. Thérèse retired to the Belgian convent, and Adolphe, the possessor of a few thousand francs, the remains of his mother's small fortune, returned to his studio and to the life he had chosen.

The success and duration of a career of this sort is in exact proportion to the amount

of capital, real or assumed, invested in it.
Monsieur Linders' capital was very small;
his francs and credit both were soon exhausted, and he began to find that making-
believe to paint pictures was hardly a paying
business. He tried to take portraits, attempt-
ed etching, gambled, and, finally, being more
in debt than he could well afford, disappeared
from the Paris world for a number of years,
and for a long space was known and heard
of no more. It was indeed affirmed in his
circle of acquaintance that he had been seen
playing a fiddle at one of the cheap theatres;
that he had been recognized in the dress
of a fiacre-driver, and in that of a waiter
at a Café Chantant: but these reports
were idly spread, and wanted confirmation.
They might or might not have been true.
M. Linders never cared to talk much of
those seven or eight years in which he had
effaced himself, as it were, from society; but

it may be imagined that he went through some strange experiences in a life which was a struggle for bare existence. Respectable ways of gaining a livelihood he ever held in aversion; and it was not, therefore, to be expected that a foolish and unprofitable pride would interfere to prevent his using any means not absolutely criminal in order to reach any desired end.

At length, however, he emerged from obscurity, and rose once more to the surface of society; and one of his old acquaintance, who encountered him at Homburg, returned marvelling to Paris to relate that he had seen Adolphe Linders winning fabulous sums at *trente-et-quarante*, that he was decently clothed, had a magnificent suite of apartments at one of the first hotels, and an English wife of wondrous beauty. Monsieur Linders had, in fact, sown his wild oats, so to speak, and settled down to the business of his life.

In former days, gambling had been a passion with him—too much so, indeed, to admit of his playing with any great success; he had been apt to lose both temper and skill. Time, however, while increasing this passion for play, till it gradually became a necessity of his life, had taught him to bring to bear upon it all the ability which would have eminently fitted him for some more praiseworthy employment. Formerly he had indulged in it as a diversion; now it became a serious business, which he prosecuted with a cool head, determined will, and unfailing perseverance—qualities for which few would have given him credit in the wild unsettled period of his early career. The result was highly satisfactory to himself; he was soon known as one of the most successful haunters of the German and Belgian gaming-tables; he cast off the outward aspect and manners of the Bohemian set he had once affected, and assumed the guise and dress of the gentleman he really was— at least by birth and education—and which he found at once more profitable and more congenial to his maturer tastes. He lived splendidly, and spent money freely when he had it; incurred debts with great facility when he had not—debts which he did or did not pay, as the case might be.

It was during a winter spent in Brussels that he made the acquaintance of Charles Moore, a young Englishman with tastes identical with his own, but inferior to him in ability, talents, and even in principles. A sort of partnership was formed between them, Mr. Linders undertaking most of the work, and the Englishman contributing his small fortune as capital; and not only his own, but that of his sister Magdalen, a young girl who had come abroad with her brother, the only near relation she had in the world.

M. Linders had been introduced to her,
and she, in complete ignorance of the real
character of either him or her brother
Charles, had, with all the simplicity of
eighteen, straightway fallen in love with the
handsome gentlemanlike man, who, on his
side, made no secret of the impresson produced on him by the great loveliness of the
English girl.   Moore, who was a thoroughly
heartless scamp, had not the least compunction in agreeing to a marriage between his
sister and this man, with whose character
and mode of life he was perfectly well
acquainted ; indeed, it suited his views so
well, that he did what lay in his power to
forward it.   There were no difficulties in
the way ; the two were almost alone in the
world. He had been left her sole guardian
by their old father, who had died a twelvemonth before ; and she, trusting her brother
entirely, was glad to leave everything in his

hands. The marriage was accomplished with all possible speed, and it was not till nearly two months later that an accident revealed to Magdalen Linders, what indeed in any case she must have discovered before long—what manner of man this was she had got for her husband.

Then she did not pine away, nor sicken with despair, being of a great courage, strong to bear evil and misfortune, and not made of the stuff that gives way under cruel deception and disappointment. She uttered only one reproach—

" You should have told me of all this, Adolphe," she said.

" You would not have married me," he answered gloomily.

" I—I do not know. Ah, I loved you so much, and so truly !"

And she did love him still; and clung to him to the last, but not the less was she broken-hearted, so far as any enjoyment of life was concerned; and her husband saw it. All sense of rejoicing seemed to die out of her heart for ever. She hated the splendour with which he sometimes surrounded her, even more than the paltry shifts and expedients to which at other times they had to resort, when he had spent all his money, and there was no more forthcoming for the moment; she wept when her children were born, thinking of the iniquity of the world they had entered; and when her two little boys died one after the other, there was almost a sense of relief mixed with the bitterness of her sorrow, as she reflected on the father she could not have taught them to respect, and on the abject evil and misery from which she could not have shielded them.

As for M. Linders, he at once adored and neglected his wife, as was the nature of

the man ; that is, he adored her theoreti-
cally for her rare beauty, but neglected her
practically, when, after a few months of
married life, he saw her bloom fading, and
her animation vanish, in the utter despond-
ency which had seized her, and which found
its outward expression in a certain studied
composure and coldness of manner. There
soon came a time when he would have willingly
freed himself altogether from the constraint
of her presence. He travelled almost in-
cessantly, spending the summer and autumn at the German watering-places ; the
winter in France, or Belgium, or Italy ; and
he would sometimes propose that she should
remain at a Paris hotel till he could return to her. In the first years after their
marriage she objected vehemently. She
was so young, so unused to solitude, that
she felt a certain terror at the prospect of
being left alone ; and, moreover, she still

clung with a sort of desperation to her girl-
ish illusions, and, loving her husband, could
not cease to believe in his love for her. She
had plans, too, for reforming him, and for
a long time would not allow herself to be
convinced of their utter vanity and hope-
lessness. After the death of her little boys,
however, she became more indifferent, or
more resigned. And so it came to pass
that when she had been married about six
years, and four months after her third child
was born, Madame Linders died, alone at a
Paris hotel, with no one near her but the
doctor, her baby's nurse, and the woman of
the house. She had dictated a few words
to tell her husband, who was then in Germany, that she was dying; and, stricken
with a horrible remorse, he had travelled
with all possible haste to Paris, and arrived at daybreak one morning to find that
his wife had died the evening before.

Madame Linders' death had been caused by a fever, under which she had sunk rapidly at last. There had been no question of heart-breaking or pining grief here—so her husband thought with a sort of satisfaction even then, as he remembered his sister's words of bitter reproach over their mother's death-bed; and yet not the less, as he looked at his dead wife's face, did the reflection force itself upon him, that he had made the misery instead of the happiness of her life. He was a man who had accustomed himself to view things from the hardest and most practical point of view; and from such a view his marriage had been rather a failure than otherwise, since the memory of the little fortune she had brought with her had vanished with the fortune itself. But it had not been altogether for money that he had married her; he had been in love with her at one time, and that time repeated itself,

with a pertinacity not to be shaken off, as
he stood now in her silent presence.

Whatever his feelings may have been,
however, they found no expression then.
He turned sharply on the women standing
round, who had already, after the fashion
of womankind, contrived, without speaking,
to let him know their opinion of a man
who had left his wife alone for six months
at an hotel, whilst he went and amused himself. He scarcely glanced at the small
daughter, now presented to him for the
first time ; and he bade Madame Lavaux,
the mistress of the hotel, " make haste and
finish with all that," when, with tearful
voice, and discursive minuteness, she related to him the history of his wife's last
days. He made all necessary arrangements ;
took possession of Madame Linders' watch
and few trinkets ; himself superintended the
packing of her clothes and other trifling

properties into a large trunk, which he
left in Madame Lavaux' charge; attended
the funeral on the following day; and
immediately on his return from it, or-
dered a fiacre to be in readiness to con-
vey him to the railway station, as he was
going to quit Paris immediately. He was
on the point of departure, when he was
confronted by Madame Lavaux and the
nurse bearing the infant, who begged to
know if he had any directions to leave concerning his child.

"Madame," he answered, addressing the
landlady, "I entrust all these matters to
you; see that the child is properly pro-
vided for, and I will send the requisite
money."

"We had arranged that her nurse should
take her away to her own home in the
country," said Madame Lavaux.

"That will do," he answered; and was

about to leave the room, when the nurse, an honest country-woman, interposed once more, to inquire where she should write to Monsieur to give him tidings of his little daughter.

"I want none," he replied. "You can apply here to Madame for money if the child lives ; if it dies she will let me know, and I need send no more." And so saying, he strode out of the room, leaving the women with hands and eyes uplifted at the hard-hearted conduct of the father.

For nearly two years M. Linders was absent from Paris, wandering about, as his habit was, from one town to another, a free man, as he would himself have expressed it, except for the one tie which he acknowledged only in the sums of money he sent from time to time, with sufficient liberality, to Madame Lavaux. No news reached him of his child, and he demanded none.

But about twenty months after his wife's death, business obliged him to go for a few weeks to Paris; and finding himself with a leisure day on his hands, it occurred to him, with a sudden impulse, to spend it in the country and go and see his little girl. He ascertained from Madame Lavaux where she was, and went.

The woman with whom little Madeleine had been placed lived about fifteen miles from Paris, in a small village perched half-way up a steep hill, from the foot of which stretched a wide plain, where the Seine wound slowly amongst trees and meadows and scattered villages. The house to which M. Linders was directed stood a little apart from the others, near the road-side, but separated from it by a strip of garden, planted with herbs and a patch of vines; and as he opened the gate, he came at once upon a pretty little picture of a child of two

years, in a quaint, short-waisted, long-skirt-
ed pinafore, toddling about, playing at hide-
and-seek among the tall poles and trailing
tendrils, and kept within safe limits by a
pair of leading-strings passed round the
arm of a woman who sat in the shade of
the doorway knitting. As M. Linders came
up the narrow pathway she ran towards
him to the utmost extent of her tether,
uttering little joyous inarticulate cries, and
bubbling over with the happy instinctive
laughter of a child whose consciousness is
bounded by its glad surroundings.

When, in moments of pseudo remorse,
which would come upon him from time to
time, it occurred to M. Linders to reflect
upon his misdeeds, and adopt an apologetic
tone concerning them, he was wont to pro-
pound a singular theory respecting his life,
averring, in general terms, that it had been
spoilt by women,—a speech more epigram-

matic, perhaps, than accurate, since of the two women who had loved him best, his mother and his wife, he had broken the heart of the one, and ruined the happiness of the other. And yet it was not without its grain of meaning, however false and distorted; for M. Linders, who was not more consistent than the rest of mankind, had, by some queer anomaly, along with all his hardness, and recklessness, and selfishness, a capacity for affection after his own fashion, and an odd sensitiveness to the praise and blame of those women whom he cared for and respected which did not originate merely in vanity and love of applause. He had been fond of his mother, though he had ignored her wishes and abused her generosity; and he had hated his sister Thérèse, because he imagined that she had come between them. Their reproaches had been unbearable to him, and though his wife had never blamed him in words, there had been a mute upbraiding in her mournful looks and dejected spirits, which he had resented as a wrong done to the love he had once felt for her. In the absence of many subjects for self-congratulation, he rather piqued himself on a warm heart and sensitive feelings, and chose to consider them ill-requited by the cold words and sad glances of those whose happiness he was destroying. The idea that he should set matters straight by adjusting his life to meet their preconceived notions of right and wrong, would have appeared to him highly absurd; but he considered them unreasonable and himself ill-used when they refused to give their approbation to his proceedings, and this idea of ill-usage and unreasonableness he was willing to encourage, as it enabled him to shift the responsibility of their unhappiness from his own shoulders on to theirs, and to deaden the sense of remorse which would make itself felt from time to time. For in the worst of men, they say, there still lingers some touch of kindly human feeling, and M. Linders, though amongst the most worthless, was not perhaps absolutely the worst of men. He was selfish enough to inflict any amount of pain, yet not hardened enough to look unmoved on his victims. He had, in truth, taken both their misery and their reproaches to heart ; and sometimes, especially since his wife's death, he had surprised in himself a strange, unaccountable desire for a love that should be true and pure, but which, ignorant of, or ignoring his errors, should be content to care for him and believe in him just as he was : such a love as his wife might, perhaps, have given him in her single month of unconscious happiness. It was a longing fitful, and not defined in words, but a real sentiment all the same, not a sentimentality ; and, imperfect as it was in scope and tendency, it expressed the best part of the man's nature. He despised it, and crushed it down; but it lay latent, ready to be kindled by a touch.

And here was a small piece of womankind belonging to him, who could upbraid by neither word nor look, who ran towards him confidently, stretching out tiny hands to clutch at his shining gold chain, and gazing up in his face with great brown eyes, that recalled to him those of her dead mother, when she had first known and learnt to love him. Had Madelon been a shy, plain child—had she hidden her face, and run from him screaming to her nurse, as children are so wont to do, he would then and there have paid the money he had brought with him as the ostensible cause of his visit, and gone on his way, thinking no more about her for another two years perhaps. But Madelon had no thought of shyness with the tall fair handsome man who had taken her fancy; she stood for a moment in the pathway before him, balancing herself on tiptoe with uplifted arms, confident in the hope of being taken up; and, as the woman recognizing M. Linders, came forward and bade the child run to Papa, with a sudden unaccustomed emotion of tenderness, almost pathetic in such a man, he stooped down and raised her in his arms.

As he travelled back to Paris that day, M. Linders formed a plan which he lost no time in carrying, partially, at least, into execution. During the next twelvemonth he spent much of his time in Paris, and went frequently to see his small daughter, never without some gift to win her heart, till the child came to regard his pocket as the inexhaustible source of boundless surprises, in the shape of toys and cakes and bonbons. It was not long before she was devoted to her father, and, her nurse dying when she was a little more than three years old, M. Linders resolved at once to carry out his idea, and, instead of placing her with any one else, take possession of her himself. He removed her accordingly from the country to Paris, engaged a *bonne*, and henceforth Madelon accompanied him wherever he went.

CHAPTER V.

MONSIEUR LINDERS' SYSTEM.

MY little lady had given Horace Graham a tolerably correct impression of her life as they had talked together in the moonlight at Chaudfontaine. When M. Linders took her home with him—if that may be called home which consisted of wanderings from one hotel to another—it was with certain fixed ideas concerning her, which he began by realizing with the success that not unfrequently attended his ideas when he set himself with a will to work them out. His child's love and trust he had already gained, as she had won suddenly for herself a place in his heart, and he started with the determination that these relations between them should never be disturbed. She should be educated for himself; she should be brought up to see with his eyes, to adopt his views; she should be taught no troublesome standard of right and wrong by which to measure him and find wanting; no cold shadow of doubt and reproach should ever rise between them and force them asunder; and above all, he would make her happy—she for one should never turn on him and say, " See, my life is ruined, and it is you who have done it!" She should know no life, no aims, no wishes but his; but that life should be so free from care and sorrow that for once he would be able to congratulate himself on having made the happiness, instead of the misery, of some one whom he loved and who loved him.

These were the ideas that M. Linders entertained concerning Madelon, expressing them to himself in thoughts and language half genuine, half sentimental, as was his nature. But his love for his child was genuine enough; and for the fulfilment of his purpose he was willing to sacrifice much, devoting himself to her, and giving up time, comfort, and even money, for the sake of this one small being whom in all the world he loved, and who was to be taught to love him. He took her about with him; she associated with his companions; he familiarized her with all his proceedings, and she came in consequence to look upon their mode of life as being as much a matter of course, and a part of the great system of things, as the child does who sees her father go out to plough every day, or mount the pulpit every

Sunday to preach his sermon. Of course she did not understand it all; it was his one object in life that she should not; and fondly as he loved his little Madelon, he did not scruple to make her welfare subordinate to his own views. He was careful to keep her within the shady bounds of that world of no doubtful character, which he found wherever he went, hovering on the borders of the world of avowed honesty and respectability, jealously guarding her from every counter-influence, however good or beneficial. He would not send her to school, was half unwilling, indeed, that she should be educated in any way, lest she should come to the knowledge of good and evil, which he so carefully hid from her; and he even dismissed her good, kind-hearted *bonne*, on overhearing her instruct the child, who could then hardly speak

plain, in some little hymn or prayer, or
pious story, such as nurses delight in
teaching their charges. After that he took
care of her himself with the assistance of
friendly landladies at the hotels he fre-
quented, who all took an interest in and
were kind to the little motherless girl, but
were too busy to have any time to spend
in teaching her, or enlarging her ideas ; and
indeed all the world conspired to carry out
M. Linders' plan; for who would have cared,
even had it been possible, to undertake the
ungracious task of opening the eyes of a
child to the real character of a father whom
she loved and believed in so implicitly?
And she was so happy, too!   Setting aside
any possible injury he might be doing her,
M. Linders was the most devoted of fathers,
loving and caring for her most tenderly,
and thinking himself well repaid by the

clinging grasp of her small hand, by the
spring of joy with which she welcomed
him after any absence, by her gleeful voice
and laughter, her perfect trust and confidence in him.

There must have been something good and
true about this man, roué and gambler
though he was, that, somehow, he himself
and those around him had missed hitherto,
but that sprang willingly into life when appealed to by the innocent faith, the undoubt-
ing love of his little child. Thus much
Madelon all unconsciously accomplished, but
more than this she could not do. M. Linders
did not become a reformed character for
her sake; he had never had any particular
principles, and Madelon's loving innocence,
which aroused all his best emotions, had no
power to stir in him any noble motives or
high aspirations, which, if they existed at

all, were buried too deep to be awakened
by the touch of her small hand. His misdeeds had never occasioned him much
uneasiness, except as they had affected
the conduct of others towards himself;
and he had no reproaches, expressed or
implied, to fear from Madelon. " No one
had ever so believed in him before!" he
would sigh, with a feeling not without a
certain pathos in its way, though with the
ring of false sentiment characteristic of the
man, and with an apparent want of perception that it was ignorance rather than belief
that was in question. Madelon believed indeed in his love, for it answered readily to
her daily and hourly appeals, but she cannot be said to have believed in his honour
and integrity, for she can hardly have
known what they meant, and she made no
claims upon *them.* It was, perhaps, happy

for her that the day when she should have occasion to do so never arrived.

She was not left quite uneducated, however; her father taught her after his own fashion, and she gained a good deal of practical knowledge in their many wanderings. When she was six years old she could talk almost as many languages, could dance, and could sing a variety of songs with the sweetest, truest little voice; and by the time she was eight or nine, she had learned both to write and read, though M. Linders took care that her range of literature should be limited, and chiefly confined to books of fairy-tales, in which no examples drawn from real life could be found, to correct and confuse the the single-sided views she received from him. This was almost the extent of her learning, but she picked up all sorts of odd bits of information, in the queer mixed society which M. Linders seemed everywhere to gather round him, and which appeared to consist of waifs and strays from every grade of society—from reckless young English mi-lords, Russian princes and Polish counts, *soi-disant*, down to German students and penniless artists.

It was, no doubt, fortunate, even at this early age, that Madelon's little pale face, with its wide-open brown eyes, had none of the prettiness belonging to the rosy-cheeked, blue-eyed, golden-haired type of beauty, and that she thus escaped a world of flattery and nonsense.   She was silent too in company, as a rule, keeping her chatter and laughter, for the most part, till she was alone with her father, and content sometimes to sit as quiet as a mouse for a whole evening, watching what was going on around her; she was too much accustomed to strangers ever to feel shy with them, but she cared little for them, unless, as in Horace Graham's case, they happened to take her fancy.

It must not be imagined, however, that M. Linders was quite without conscience as regarded his child; there were some people with whom he took care that she should not associate, some society into which he never took her. Many an evening did Madelon spend happily enough while her father was out, in the snug little parlours of the hotels, where Madame, the landlady, would be doing up her accounts perhaps, and Monsieur, the landlord, reposing after the exertions of the day; whilst Mademoiselle Madelon, seated at the table, would build card-houses, or play at dominoes, and eat galette and confitures to her heart's content. Here, too, she would get queer little glimpses into life—hearing very likely how Monsieur

B. had 'made off without paying his bill, or how those trunks that Madame la Comtesse C. had left eighteen months ago, as a pledge of her return, had been opened at last, and been found to contain nothing but old clothes, fit for the rag-market; how a few francs might be advantageously added on here and there in the bill for the rich English family at the *premier*; how the gentleman known as No. 5 was looked upon as a suspicious character; and how Pierre the waiter had been set to watch the door of No. 8, who had spent three months in the house without paying a sou, and was daily suspected of attempting to abscond. All these, and a dozen similar stories, and half the gossip of the town, would come buzzing round Madelon's ears as she sat gravely balancing one card on the top of the other. She heard and comprehended them with such comprehension as was in her; and no doubt they modified in some degree her

childish views of life, which in these early
years was presented to her, poor child!
under no very sublime or elevated aspect; but they had little interest for her,
and she paid small heed to them.   In
truth, her passionate love for her father
was, no doubt, at this time her great pre-
servative and safeguard, ennobling her,
as every pure unselfish passion must en-
noble, and by absorbing her thoughts and
heart, acting as a charm against many an
unworthy influence around her.   The first
sound of his footstep outside was enough to
put both stories and gossip out of her head,
and was the signal for her to spring from
her chair, and rush into the passage to meet
him ; and a few minutes after they would be
seated together in their room upstairs, she
nestling on his knee most likely, with her
arm tight round his neck, while he recounted
the adventures of the evening.   His purse

would be brought out, and it was Madelon's special privilege and treat to pour out the contents on the table and count them over. If M. Linders had won, it was a little fête for both—calculations as to how it should be spent, where they should go the next day, what new toy, or frock, or trinket should be bought ; if he had lost, there would be a moment of discouragement perhaps, and then Madelon would say,

" It does not signify, papa, does it ?—you will win to-morrow, you know."

As for M. Linders, the thought of the little, eager innocent face that would greet his return home was the brightest and purest vision that lighted his dark and wayward life, and he appealed to his child's sympathy and encouragement in a way that had something touching in it, showing as it did the gentler side of a man who was always reckless, and could be hard and merciless enough

sometimes ; but he was never anything but
tender with his little Madelon, and one can
fancy the two sitting together, as she counts
over the little gold pieces shining in the
candlelight.   Once, not long after his marriage, he had appealed to his wife in the
same way, when, after an unusual run of
luck, he had returned in triumph with his
winnings.   She, poor girl, looked first at
them and then at him, with a piteous little
attempt at a smile ; then suddenly burst into
tears, and turned away.   It was the first and
last time he tried to win her sympathy in
these matters, and was, perhaps, the beginning of the sort of estrangement that grew
up between them.

These were happy evenings, Madelon
thought, but she found those happier still
when her father was at home, generally
with one or two men who would come in to
play cards with him.   They were always

good-natured and kind to the little girl who
sat so still and close to her father's side,
watching the game with her quick, intelli-
gent eyes; though some of them, foolish
smooth-faced lads, perhaps, would go away
cursing the fate that had ever led them across
M. Linders' path, and carrying an undying
hatred in their hearts for the handsome
courteous man who had enticed them on to
ruin.   How M. Linders lured these poor
birds into the snare, and by what means he
plucked them when there, Madelon never
knew; all that belonged to the darker
side of his character, which she never fully
understood, and on which, for her sake, we
will not dwell.

Most of all, however, did Madelon enjoy
being at the German watering-places, for
then she went out with her father constantly.
The fair-haired, brown-eyed little girl was
almost as well known in the Kursaals of

Homburg and Wiesbaden as the famous
gambler himself, as evening after evening
they entered the great lighted salons together, and took their places amongst the
motley crowd gathered round the long
green tables. There she would remain contented for hours, sometimes sitting on his
knee, sometimes herself staking a florin or
two—"to change the luck," M. Linders would
say laughingly,—sometimes wearied out,
curled up fast asleep in a corner of one of
the sofas. Then there were the theatres,
to which her father often took her, and
where, with delighted, wondering eyes,
she made acquaintance with most of the
best operas, and learnt to sing half Bel-
lini's and Weber's music in her clear little voice. More than once, too, she was
taken behind the scenes, where she saw so
much of the mysteries of stage-working and
carpentering as would have destroyed the

illusions of an older person; but it did not make much difference to her; the next time she found herself in the stalls or balcony she forgot all about what was going on behind, and was as much enchanted as ever with the fine results prepared for the public gaze.

On other nights there would be the balls, always a supreme enjoyment. It must be owned that Madelon took great pleasure in seeing her small person arrayed in a smart frock; and she was never weary of admiring the big rooms with their gilded furniture, and mirrors, and brilliant lights, and polished floors, where a crowd of gay people would be twirling about to the sound of the music. She danced like a little fairy, too, with pure delight in the mere motion, was never tired, and rarely sat down; for Mademoiselle, who generally held herself rather aloof from strangers, would be pleased

on these occasions to put on a little winning
graciousness, giving her hand with the air of
a small princess to any one soliciting the
honour of a dance ; and she was seldom
without some tall partner, attracted by her
gentillesse and naïve prattle—a moustached
Austrian or Prussian officer, perhaps, in
white or blue uniform, or one of her counts
or barons, with a bit of ribbon dangling from
his button-hole ; or, if all else failed, there
was always her father, who was ever ready
to indulge her in any of her fancies, and
never resisted her coaxing pleading for one
more dance.

These were the evenings ; for the days
there were pleasures enough too, though of
a simpler kind, and more profitable, perhaps, for our poor little Madelon, in her
gay unconscious dance through that mad
Vanity Fair, innocent though it was for her
as yet.

Except on some special emergency, M. Linders rarely went to the gambling tables during the day. He had a theory that daylight was prejudicial to his prosperity, and that it was only at night that he could play there with any fair chance of success ; but he not unfrequently had other business of a similar nature on hand to occupy his mornings and afternoons ; and when he was engaged or absent, Madelon, with the happy adaptability of a solitary child, had no difficulty in amusing herself alone with her toys, and picture-books, and dolls. At other times, when her father was at leisure, there would be walks with him, long afternoons spent in the gay Kursaal gardens, listening to the bands of music ; and on idle days, which with M. Linders were neither few nor far between, excursions perhaps into the country, sometimes the two alone, but more frequently accompanied by one or two of

M. Linders' companions. There they would
dine at some rustic Gasthof, and afterwards,
whilst her father and his friends smoked,
drank their Rhine wine, and brought out
the inevitable cards and dice in the shady,
vine-trellised garden, Madelon, wandering
about here and there, in and out, through
yard and court, and garden and kitchen,
poking her small nose everywhere, gained
much primary information on many subjects,
from the growing of cabbages to the making
sauerkraut—from the laying of eggs by ever-
hopeful hens, to their final fulfilment of a
ruthless destiny in a frying-pan. In return,
she was not unwilling to impart to the good
Hausfrau, and her troop of little ones and
retainers, many details concerning her town
life ; and might sometimes be found, perched
on the kitchen table, relating long histories
to an admiring audience, in which the blue

silk frocks and tall partners made no small figure, one may be sure.

It was a golden childhood. Even in after years, when, reading the history of these early days in a new light, she suffered a pang for almost every pleasure she had then enjoyed, even then Madelon maintained that her childhood had been one of unclouded happiness, such as few children know. The sudden changes of fortune, from splendour to poverty of the shabbiest description, the reckless, dishonest expenditure, and the endless debts consequent on it; the means —doubtful to say the least of them—employed by M. Linders for procuring money; the sense of alienation from all that is best, and noblest, and truest in life;—all these, which had gone far to make up the sum of her mother's misery, affected our Madelon hardly at all. Some of them she did

not know of; the rest she took as a matter of course.   In truth, it mattered little
to her whether they lived in a big hotel
or a little one; whether the debts were
paid or unpaid; whether money were
forthcoming or not; she never felt the
want of it, we may be sure.   If she did not
have some promised fête or amusement on
one day, it was certain to come on another;
and even the one or two occasions on which
M. Linders, absolutely unable to leave an
hotel until he had paid part of what he owed
there, had been obliged to confiscate everything, caused her no uneasiness.   The next
week, very likely, she had other trinkets
and knick-knacks, newer and prettier; and
indeed, so long as she had her father, she
cared for little else.   In any small childish
misfortune or ailment she had but to run
to him to find help, and sympathy, and
caresses; and she had no grief or care in

these first years for which these were not a sufficient remedy.

Amidst all the miserable failures, and more unworthy successes of a wasted life, M. Linders gained at least one legitimate triumph, when he won his child's undying love and gratitude. All her life long, one may fancy, would Madelon cherish the remembrance of his unceasing tenderness, of his unwearying love for his little girl, which showed itself in a thousand different ways, and which, with one warm, loving little heart, at any rate, would ever go far to cover a multitude of sins. The only drawback to her perfect content in these early days was the presence of her uncle Charles, whom she could not bear, and who, for his part, looked upon her as a mere encumbrance, and her being with them at all as a piece of fatuity on the part of his brother-in-law. There were constant skir-

mishes between them while they were together; but even these ceased after a time, for
Moore, who, ever since his sister's marriage,
had clung fitfully to M. Linders, as a luckier
and more prosperous man that himself was
accustomed to be absent on his own account
for months together, and during one of
these solitary journeys that he died, about
two years after Horace Graham had seen
him at Chaudfontaine.   Henceforth Madelon and her father were alone.

Madelon, then, by the time she was eight
years old, had learnt to sing, dance, speak
several languages, to write, to play *rouge et
noir*, and *roulette*, and indeed *piquet* and
écarté, too, to great perfection, and to read
books of fairy tales.   At ten years old, her
education was still at the same point; and it
must be owned that, however varied and
sufficient for the purposes of the moment, it

left open a wide field for labour in future
years; though M. Linders appeared perfectly satisfied with the results of his teaching so far, and showed no particular desire
to enlarge her ideas upon any point. As
for religion, no wild Arab of our London
streets ever knew or heard less about it than
did our little Madelon ; or was left more
utterly uninstructed in its simplest truths
and dogmas. What M. Linders' religious beliefs were, or whether he had any at all, we
need not inquire. He at least took care
that none should be instilled into his child's
mind ; feeling, probably, that under whatever form they were presented to her, they
would assuredly clash sooner or later with
his peculiar system of education. For himself, his opinions on such matters were expressed when occasion arose, only in certain unvarying and vehement declamations

against priests and nuns—the latter particularly, where his general sense of aversion
to a class in the abstract, became specific
and definite, when he looked upon that
class as represented in the person of his sister Thérèse.

Of the outward forms and ceremonies of
religion Madelon could not, indeed, remain
entirely ignorant, living constantly, as she
did, in Roman Catholic countries; but her
very familiarity with these from her baby-
hood robbed them in great measure of the
interest they might otherwise have excited
in her mind, and their significance she was
never taught to understand. As a rule, a
child must have its attention drawn in some
particular way to its every-day surroundings,
or they must strike it in some new and un-
familiar light, before they rouse more than a
passing curiosity; and though Madelon would
sometimes question her father as to the mean-

ing and intention of this or that procession passing along the streets, he found no difficulty in putting her off with vague answers. It was a wedding or a funeral, he would say, or connected with some other ordinary event, which Madelon knew to be of daily recurrence; though none such had as yet had part in the economy of her small world; and priests, and nuns, and monks became classed, without difficulty, in her mind, with doctors and soldiers, and the mass of people generally, who made money in a different way from her father, with whom, therefore, she seldom came into personal contact, and with whom she had little to do—money making being still her one idea of the aim and business of life.

The first time, however, that she ever entered a church, when she was little more than nine years old, was an experience in her life, and this was the occasion of it. It was in a French provincial town, where M. Linders had stopped for a day on business— only for one day, but that Madelon was to spend for the most part alone; for her father, occupied with his affairs, was obliged to go out very early, and leave her to her own devices; and very dull she found them, after the first hour or two. She was a child of many resources, it is true, but these will come to an end when a little girl of nine years old, with books and dolls all packed up, has to amuse herself for ever so many hours in a dull country hotel, an hotel, too, which was quite strange to her, and where she could not, therefore, fall back upon the society and conversation of a friendly landlady. Madelon wandered up-stairs and downstairs, looked out of all the windows she could get at, and at last stood leaning against the hall-door, which opened on to the front courtyard. It was very quiet and very dull, nothing moving anywhere; no one crossed the square, sunny space, paved with little stones, and adorned with the usual round-topped trees, in green boxes. Inside the house there was an occasional clatter of plates and dishes, or the resonant nasal cry of " Auguste," or " Henri," from one or other of the servants, but that was all. Madelon found it too tiresome; the *porte-cochère* stood half open, she crossed the court-yard and peeped out. She saw a quiet, sunny street, with not much more life or movement than there was within, but still a little better. Over the high walls surround-ing the houses opposite green trees were waving; at one end of the street there was the gleam of a river, a bridge, and a row of poplars; the other end she could not see, for the street made a bend, and a fountain with dribbling water filled up the angle. Presently a little boy in a blue blouse, and a little girl with a tight round white cap, came up to the stone basin, each with a pitcher to fill; they were a long time about it, for what could be pleasanter, on this hot summer morning, than to stand dabbling one's fingers in the cool water? Madelon watched them till she became possessed with an irresistible desire to do the same. It was only a few steps off, and though she was strictly forbidden by her father ever to go out alone, still—she had so seldom an opportunity of being naughty, that her present consciousness of disobedience rather added, perhaps, to the zest of the adventure. She would go just for this once—and in another moment she was out in the street. The little boy and girl fled with full pitchers as she came up to the fountain, suddenly awakened to a sense of the waste of time in which they had been indulging; but that made no difference to Madelon; she stood gazing with mute admiration at the open-mouthed monsters, from whose wide jaws the water trickled into the basin below; and then she held her hands to catch the drops till they were quite cold, and thought it the best play she had ever known. By-and-by, however, she began to look about her in search of further excitement, and, emboldened by success, turned the corner of the street, and ventured out of sight of the hotel. On one side large *porte-cochères* at intervals, shutting in the white, green-shuttered houses that appeared beyond; on the other a long, high, blank wall, with nothing to be seen above it, and one small arched doorway about half-way down. This was the shady side; and Madelon, crossing over to it, arrived at the arched door, and stood for a moment contemplating it, wondering what could be inside.

She was not left long in doubt, for two

priests crossed the road, and pushed open
the door, without seeing the child, who,
urged by a spirit of curiosity, crept un-
noticed after them, and suddenly found herself in a cloister, running round a quadrangle, on one side of which rose the walls
and spires and buttresses of a great church;
in the centre a carefully kept space of
smooth grass.   Madelon stood for a moment
motionless with delight; it reminded her of
a scene in some opera or play to which she
had been in Paris with her father, but, oh !
how much more beautiful, and all real !
The sunlight streamed through the tracery
of the cloisters, and fell chequered with
sharp shadows on the pavement; the bright
blue sky was crossed with pinnacles and
spires, and there was an echo of music from
the church which lured her on.   The two
priests walked quickly along, she followed,

and all three entered the building by a side
door together.

A vast, dim church, with long aisles and
lofty pillars, which seemed to Madeleine's
unpractised eye, fresh from the outer glare,
to vanish in infinite mysterious gloom; a
blaze of light at the far-off high altar, with
its priests, and incense, and gorgeous garments, and tall candles; on every side
shrines and tapers, and pictures, awful, agon-
ised, compassionate Saviours, sad, tender
Madonnas; a great silent multitude of
kneeling people; and, above all, the organ
pealing out, wave after wave of sound,
which seemed to strike her, surround her,
thrill her with a sense of—what? What
was it all? What did it all mean? An
awful instinct suddenly woke in the child's
heart, painfully struggling with inarticulate
cries, as it were, to make itself understood,

even to herself. Wholly inarticulate, for she
had been taught no words that could express,
however feebly, these vague yearnings, these
unutterable longings, suddenly stirring in
her heart. This wonderful, solemn music,
this place, so strange, so separate from any
other she had known, what was it? what did
it all mean ?   Ah, yes, what did it all mean ?
A little girl, no older than herself, who
knelt close by the door, with careless eyes
that roamed everywhere, and stared wondering at Madelon's cotton frock and rough uncovered little head, could have explained it
all very well ; she had a fine gilt prayer-
book in her hand, and knew most of her
Catechism, and could have related the history of all the saints in the church ; she did
not find it at all impressive, though she
liked coming well enough on these grand
fête-days, when everyone wore their best

clothes, and she could put on her very newest frock.   But our little stray Madelon, who
knew of none of all these things, could find
nothing better to do at last than to creep
into a dark corner, between a side chapel
and a confessional, crouch down, and begin
to sob with all her heart.

Presently the music ceased, and the
people went pouring out of the great doors
of the church. Madelon, roused by the movement around her, looked up, dried her eyes,
and came out of her corner; then, following
the stream, found herself once more outside,
not in the cloister by the door of which
she had entered, but at the top of a wide
flight of steps, leading down to a large
sunny Place, surrounded with houses, where
a fair was going on. She was fairly bewildered; she had never been in the town before,
and though, in fact, not very far from the

hotel where she was staying, she felt completely lost.

As she stood still for a moment, in the midst of the dispersing crowd, looking scared and dazed enough very likely, she once more attracted the attention of the little girl who had been kneeling near her in the church, and who now pointed her out to her parents, good, substantial-looking *bourgeois*.

"*Comme elle a l'air drôle*," said the child, "with her hair all rough, and that old cotton frock!"

"She looks as if she had lost someone," says the kindly mother. "I will ask her."

"No, she had not lost anyone," Madelon said, in answer to her inquiries, "but she did not know where she was; could Madame tell her the way to the Hôtel de l'Aigle d'Or?"

"It is quite near," Madame answered;

"we are going that way ; if you like to come with us, we will show it to you."

So Madelon followed the three down the broad steps, and out into the Place, where she looked a queer little figure enough, perhaps, in the midst of all the gay holiday-folk who were gathered round the booths and stalls. She did not concern herself about that, however, for her mind was still full of what she had seen and heard in the church; and she walked on silently, till presently Madame, with some natural curiosity as to this small waif and stray she had picked up, said, "Are you staying at the hotel, *ma petite ?*"

"Yes," answered Madelon, "we came there last night."

"And how was it you went to church all alone ?"

"Papa had to go out," says Madelon, getting rather red and confused, "and I was so dull by myself, and I—I went out into the street, and got into the church by a little door at the side—not that other one we came out at just now; so I did not know where I was, nor the way back again."

"Then you are a stranger here, and have never been to the church before?" said Monsieur.

"No," said Madelon; and then, full of her own ideas, she asked abruptly—"what was everyone doing in there?"

"In there!—in the church, do you mean?"

"Yes, in the church—what was everyone doing?"

"But do you not know, then," said the mother, "that it is to-day a great fête—the fête of the Assumption?"

"No," said Madelon, "I did not know. Was that why so many people were there? What were they doing?" she persisted.

" How do you mean ?—do you not go to the *messe* every Sunday ?" said Madame, surprised.

" To the *messe !*" answered Madelon— " what is that ? I never was in a church before."

" Never in a church before !" echoed a chorus of three astonished voices, while Monsieur added—" Never in this church, you mean."

" No," answered Madelon, " it is the first time I ever went into a church at all."

" But, *mon enfant*," said the mother, " you are big enough to have gone to church long before this. Why, you must be eight or nine years old, and Nanette here went to the *grande messe* before she was five—did you not, Nanette ?"

" Yes," says Nanette, with a further sense of superiority added to that already induced by the contrast of her new white muslin frock with Madelon's somewhat limp exterior.

"And never missed it for a single Sunday or fête-day since," continued Madame, "except last year, when she had the measles."

" Do you go there every Sunday ?" asked Madelon of the child.

" Yes, every Sunday and fête-days. Would you like to see my new Paroissien? My god-father gave it to me on my last birthday."

"And is it always like to-day, with all the singing, and music, and people ?"

" Yes, always the same, only not always quite so grand, you know, because to-day is a great fête. Why don't you go to church always ?"

" She is perhaps a little Protestant," suggested the father, "and goes to the Temple. Is that not it, my child ?"

"I do not know," said Madelon, bewildered; "I never went to any Temple, and I never heard of Protestants. Papa never took me to church; but then we do not live here, you know."

"But in other churches it is the same——everywhere," cries Madame.

"What, in all the big churches in Paris, and everywhere?" said Madelon. "I did not know; I never went into them, but I will ask papa to take me there now." Then, recurring to her first difficulty, she repeated, "But what do people go there for?"

"Mais—pour prier le bon Dieu!" said the good man.

"I do not understand," said Madelon, despairingly. "What does that mean? What were the music and the lights for, and what were all the pictures about?"

"But is it, then, possible, *ma petite*, that you have had no one to teach you all these things? And on Sundays, what do you do then?" said the mother, while Nanette stared more and more at Madelon, with round eyes.

"We generally go into the country on Sundays," said Madelon. "Papa never goes to church, I am sure, or he would have taken me. I will ask him to let me go again—I like it very much." It was at this moment that they turned into the street in which stood the hotel. "Ah! there is papa," cried Madelon, rushing forward as she saw him coming towards them, and springing into his arms. He had returned to the hotel for a late *déjeûner*, and was in terrible dismay when Madelon, being sought for, was nowhere to be found. One of the waiters said he had seen her run out of the courtyard, and M. Linders was just going out to look for her.

" *Mon Dieu!* Madelon," he cried, " where, then, have you been ?"

" I ran out, papa," said Madelon, abashed. " I am very sorry—I will not do it again. I lost myself, but Monsieur and Madame here showed me the way back."

Her friendly guides stood watching the two for a moment, as, after a thousand thanks and acknowledgments, they entered the hotel together.

" It is singular," said Madame ; " he is handsome, and looks like a gentleman. How can anyone bring up a little child like that in such ignorance?   She can have no mother, *pauvre petite !*"

" What an odd little girl, Maman," cried Nanette, " never to have been to church be-fore, and not to know why people go!"

" *Chut,* Nanette !" said her father. " Thou also wouldst have known nothing, unless some good friends had taught thee." And so these kindly people went their way.

Madelon, meanwhile, was relating all her adventures to her father. He was too rejoiced at having found her again to scold her for running away; but he was greatly put out, nevertheless, as he listened to her little history. Here, then, was an emergency such as he had dimly foreseen, and done much to avoid, which yet had come upon him unawares, without fault of his, and which he was quite unprepared to meet. He did not, indeed, fully understand its importance, nor all that was passing in his child's mind; but he did perceive that she had caught a glimpse through doors he had vainly tried to keep closed to her, and that that one glance had so aroused her curiosity and interest, that it would be less easy than usual to satisfy her.

"Why do you never go to church, papa?" she was asking. "Why do you not take me? It was so beautiful, and there were such numbers of people. Why do we not go ?"

"I don't care about it myself," he answered, at last, "but you shall go again some day, *ma petite*, if you like it so much."

"May I?" said Madelon. "And will you take me, papa? What makes so many people go? Madame said they went every Sunday and *fête* day."

"I suppose they like it," answered M. Linders. "Some people go every day, and all day long—nuns, for instance, who have nothing else to do."   .

"It is, then, when people have nothing else to do that they go?" asked Madelon, misunderstanding him, with much simplicity.

"Something like it," answered M. Linders, rather grimly; then, with a momentary compunction, added, "Not precisely. They do it also, I suppose, because they think it right."

"And do you not think it right, papa? Why should they? I have seen people coming out of church before, but I never knew what it was like inside. I *may* go again some day?"

"When you are older, my child, I will take you again, perhaps."

"But that little girl Nanette, papa, was only five years old when she went first, her mother said, and I have never been at all," said Madelon, feeling rather aggrieved.

"Well, when we go to Florence next winter, Madelon, you shall visit all the churches. They are much more splendid than these, and have the most beautiful pictures, which I should like you to see."

"And will there be music, and lights, and flowers there, the same as here, papa?"

"Oh! for that, it is much the same everywhere," replied M. Linders. " People are much alike all the world over, as you will find, Madelon. Priests, and mummery, and a gaping crowd, to stare and say, ' How wonderful ! how beautiful !' as you do now, *ma petite* ; but you shall know better some day."

He spoke with a certain bitterness that Madelon did not understand, any more than she did his little speech ; but it silenced her for a moment, and then she said more timidly,

" But, papa——"

" Well, Madelon !"

" But, papa, he said—*ce Monsieur*—he said that people go to church *pour prier le bon Dieu*. What did he mean ? We often say ' *Mon Dieu*,' and I have heard them talk of *le bon Dieu* ; is that the same ? Who is He then—*le bon Dieu ?*"

M. Linders did not at once reply. Made-

lon was looking up into his face with wide-
open perplexed eyes, frowning a little with
an unusual effort of thought, with the en-
deavour to penetrate a momentous mystery,
which she instinctively felt lay somewhere,
and which she looked to him to explain;
and he *could* not give her a careless, mocking
answer; he sat staring blankly at her for a
few seconds, and then said slowly,

" I cannot tell you."

" Do you not know, papa ?"

" Yes, yes, certainly I know," he answered
hastily, and with some annoyance ; " but—in
short, Madelon, you are too young to trouble
your head about these things; you cannot
understand them possibly; when you are
older you shall have them explained to
you."

" When, papa ?"

" Oh, I don't know—one of these days,
when you are a great girl, grown up."

"And you can't tell me now?" said Madelon, a little wistfully ; "but you will let me
go to the church again before that?   Oh,
indeed it was beautiful, with the lights, and
the singing, and the music.   Do you know,
papa, it made me cry," she added, in a half
whisper.

" *Vraiment!*" said M. Linders, with some
contempt in his voice, and a slight, involun-
tary shrug of the shoulders.

The contempt was for a class of emotion
with which he had no sympathy, and for
that which he imagined had called it forth ;
not for his little Madelon, nor for her expression of it.   But the child shrank back,
blushing scarlet.   He saw his mistake, perhaps, for he drew her towards him again,
and with a tender caress and word tried to
turn her thoughts in another direction ; but
it was too late ; the impression had been
made, and could never again be effaced.

All unconsciously, with that one inadvertent word, M. Linders had raised the first slight barrier between himself and his child, had given the first shock to that confidence which he had fondly hoped was ever to exist undisturbed between them. In the most sacred hour her short life had yet known, Madeleine had appealed to him for help and sympathy, and she had been repulsed without finding either. She did not indeed view it in that light, nor believe in and love him the less; she only thought she must have been foolish; but she took well to heart the lesson that she should henceforth keep such folly to herself—as far as he was concerned, at any rate.

As for M. Linders, this little conversation left him alarmed, perplexed, uneasy. What if, after all, this small being whom he had proposed to identify, as it were, with himself, by teaching her to see with his eyes, to apprehend with his understanding, what if she were beginning to develop an independent soul, to have thoughts, notions, ideas of her own, perhaps, to look out into life with eager eyes that would penetrate beyond the narrow horizon it had pleased him to fix as her range of vision, to ask questions whose answers might lead to awkward conclusions? For the moment it seemed to him that his whole system of education, which had worked so well hitherto, was beginning to totter, ready, at any time, it might be, to fall into ruins, leaving him and his child vainly calling to each other across an ever-widening, impassable gulf. Already he foresaw as possible results all that he had most wished to avoid, and felt himself powerless to avert them; for, however ready to alienate her from good influences, and expose her to bad ones, he yet shrank from inculcating falsehood and wrong

by precept. With a boy it would have been
different, and he might have had little hesitation in bringing him up, by both precept and
example, in the way he was to go; but with
his little innocent woman-child—no, it was
impossible. She must be left to the silent and
negative teachings of surrounding influences,
and in ignorance of all others; and what if
these should fail? Perhaps he over-estimated
the immediate danger, not taking sufficiently
into account the strength and loyalty of her
affection for him; but, on the other hand,
he perhaps undervalued the depth and
force of those feelings to the consciousness
of which she had first been roused that
day. "It shall not occur again, and in
time she will forget all about it," was his
first conclusion. His second was perhaps
wiser in his generation, taking into consideration a wider range of probabilities.
"No," he reflected, "there has been an

error somewhere.   I should have accustomed Madelon to all these things, and then
she would have thought nothing of them.
Well, that shall be remedied, for she shall
go to every church in Florence, and so get
used to them."

CHAPTER VI.

AT FLORENCE.

IF we have dwelt with disproportionate
detail on the above little incident, we
must be forgiven in consideration of its
real importance to our Madeleine, marking,
as it did, the commencement of a new era
in her life. The sudden inspiration that had
kindled for a moment in the great church
died away, indeed, as newer impressions
more imperatively claimed her attention;
but the memory of it remained as a starting point to which any similar sensations
subsequently recurring might be referred,
as a phenomenon which seemed to contain

within itself the germ and possible explanation of a thousand vague aspirations, yearnings which began about this time to spring up in her mind, and which almost unconsciously linked themselves with that solemn hour the remembrance of which, after her conversation with her father, she had set apart in her own heart, to be pondered on from time to time, but in silence, —a reticence too natural and legitimate not to be followed by a hundred others of a similar kind.

M. Linders, for reasons of his own, with which we need not concern ourselves here, spent the following autumn and winter in Florence, establishing himself in an apartment for the season, contrary to his usual practice of living in hotels; and this was how it happened that Madelon made two friends who introduced quite a new element into her life, one which, under other circumstances, might hardly have entered into it as a principle of education at all. The rooms M. Linders had taken were on the third floor of a large palazzo with many occupants, where a hundred feet daily passed up and down the common staircase, the number of steps they had to tread increasing for the most part in direct proportion to their descent in the social grade which, with sufficiently imposing representatives on the first floor, reached its minimum, in point of wealth and station, in the fifth storey garret. On the same floor as Madelon and her father, but on the opposite side of the corridor, lived an American artist; and M. Linders had not been a week in the house before he recognized in him an ancient *confrère* of his old Parisian artist days, who, after many wanderings to and fro on the earth, had finally settled himself

in Florence. The old intimacy was renewed without difficulty on either side. M.
Linders was made free of the American's
atelier, and he, for his part, willingly smoked his pipe of an evening in the French-
man's little salon. He was a great black-
bearded yellow-faced fellow, with a certain
careless joviality about him, that made him
popular, though leading a not very respectable life; always extravagant, always in debt,
and not averse to a little gambling and bet-
ting when they came in his way. He was a
sufficiently congenial spirit for M. Linders
to associate with freely; but he was kind-
hearted, honourable after his own fashion,
and had redeeming points in an honest enthusiasm, in a profound conviction of the grand
possibilties of life in general, and of his art in
particular. He was no great artist, and his
business consisted mainly in making copies

of well-known pictures, which he did with great skill, so that they always commanded a ready sale in the Florence market. But he also painted a variety of original subjects, and, in unambitious moments, occasionally surprised himself by producing some charming little picture which encouraged him to persevere in this branch of his art.

This man took a great fancy to Madelon, in the first instance from hearing how prettily and deftly she spoke English; and she, after holding herself aloof in dignified reserve for three days from this new acquaintance, was suddenly won over in a visit to his *atelier*, which henceforth became to her a sort of wonderland, a treasure domain, where she might come and go as she pleased, and where, from beneath much accumulated dust, persevering fingers might extract unimagined prizes, in the shape of sketches, drawings, plaster casts, prints, and divers queer posessions of different kinds. After this, she soon became fast friends with the American, who was very kind and good-natured to her, and M. Linders' promise that she should see all the churches in Florence was fulfilled by the artist. He took her to visit both them and the galleries, showed her the famous pictures, and told her the names of their painters; and the genuine reverence with which he gazed on them, his ever-fresh enjoyment and appreciation of them, impressed her, child as she was, far more than any mere expressions of admiration or technical explanation of their merits would have done.

Sometimes, if she accompanied him to any of the churches where he happened to be copying a picture, he would leave her to wander about alone, and they were strange

weird hours that she spent in this way.
She did not indeed again assist at any of
the great church ceremonies, but the silent
spaces of these chill, grand, solemn interiors
impressed her scarcely less with a sense of
mysterious awe. Tapers twinkled in dim side
chapels, pictures and mosaics looked down
on her from above, rare footsteps echoed
along the marble pavements, silent figures
knelt about here and there, pillars, marbles,
statues gleamed, and heavy doors and curtains shut in the shadowy, echoing, silent
place from the sunshine, and blue sky, and
many coloured life without. Madelon,
wandering about in the gloom, gliding softly into every nook and corner, gazing at
tombs and decorated altars and pictures,
wondered more and more at this strange
new world in which she found herself, and
which she had no one to interpret to her.

It had a mysterious attraction for her, as
nothing had ever had before; and yet it was
almost a relief at last to escape again into
the warm, sunny out-of-door life, to walk
home with the painter through the bright
narrow streets, listening to his gay careless
talk, and lingering, perhaps, at some stall,
in the busy market-place, to buy grapes and
figs; and then to take a walk with her
father into the country, where roses nodded
at her over garden walls, and vines were
yellowing beneath the autumn sky. Her
sensitive perception of beauty and grandeur
was so much greater than her power of
grasping and comprehending them, that her
poor little mind became oppressed and
bewildered by the disproportion between
the vividness with which she received new
impressions, and her ability for seizing their
meaning.

The pictures themselves, which, before long, she learnt to delight in, and even in some sort to appreciate, were a perpetual source of perplexity to her in the unknown subjects they represented. Her want of knowledge in such matters was so complete that her American friend, who, no doubt, took it for granted that she had been brought up in the religion of the country, never even guessed at it, not imagining that a child could remain so utterly uninstructed in the simple facts and histories; and, somehow, Madelon divined this, and began to have a shy reluctance in asking questions which would betray an unsuspected ignorance. "This is such or such a Madonna," the artist would say : "there you see St. Elizabeth, and that is St. John the Baptist, you know." Or he would point out St. Agnes, or St. Cecilia, or St. Catherine, as the case might be.

" Who was St. Catherine?" Madelon ventured to ask one day.

" Did you never hear of her?" he answered. "Well then, I will tell you all about her. There were, in fact, two St. Catherines, but this one here, who, you see, has a wheel, lived long before the other. There once dwelt in Alexandria a lovely and accomplished maiden—" And he would no doubt have related to her the whole of the beautiful old mystical legend; but her father, who happened to be with them that day, interrupted him.

" Don't stuff the child's head with that nonsense," he said, and, perhaps, afterwards gave his friend a hint; for Madelon heard no more about the saints, and was left to puzzle out meanings and stories for the pictures for herself—and queer enough ones she often made, very likely. On the other hand, the American, who liked to talk to

her in his own tongue, and to make her
chatter to him in return, would tell her
many a story of the old master painters, of
Cimabue and the boy Giotto, of Lionardo da
Vinci, and half a dozen others ; old, old tales
of the days when, as we sometimes fancy
looking back through the mist of centuries,
there were giants on the earth, but all new
and fresh to our little Madelon, and with a
touch of romance and poetry about them as
told by the enthusiastic artist, which readily
seized her imagination ; indeed he himself,
with his black velvet cap, and short pipe,
and old coat, became somehow ennobled
and idealised in her simple mind by his as-
sociation through his art with the mighty
men he was teaching her to reverence.

Madelon spent much of her time in the
painter's *atelier*, for her father took it into
his head this winter to try his hand once
more at his long neglected art, and, armed

with brushes and palette, passed many of
his leisure hours in his friend's society. We
cannot accredit M. Linders with any profound penetration, or with any subtle perception of what was working in his little
daughter's mind, but with the most far-
reaching wisdom he could hardly have de-
vised better means, at this crisis in her life,
for maintaining his old hold upon her, and
keeping up the sense of sympathy between
them, which had in one instance been disturbed and endangered.

She was just beginning to be conscious of
the existence of a new and glorious world,
where money-making was, on the whole, in
abeyance, and roulette tables and croupiers
had apparently no existence at all; and the
sight of her father at his easel day after day,
at once connected him with it, as it were,
since he also could produce pictures—*tout
comme un autre.* Then M. Linders could

talk well on most subjects, and in the discussions that the two men would not unfrequently hold concerning pictures, Madelon was too young, and had too strong a conviction of her father's perfect wisdom, to discern between his mere clever knowledge of art and the American's pure love and enthusiasm ; or if, with some instinctive sense of the difference, she turned more readily to the latter for information, that was because it was his *métier* ; whereas with papa——Oh ! with papa it was only an amusement ; his business was of quite another kind.

The American amused himself by painting Madelon more than once ; and she made a famous little model, sitting still and patiently for hours to him and to her father, who had a knack of producing any number of little, affected, meretricious pictures, in the worst possible style and taste. Years afterwards, Madelon revisited the studio, where the

black-bearded friendly American, grown a
little bent and a little grey, was still stepping
backwarks and forwards before the same
easel standing in the old place ; orange and
pomegranate trees still bloomed in the windows; footsteps still passed up and down
the long corridor outside where her light
childish ones had so often echoed; the old
properties hung about on the walls; and there,
amongst dusty rolls piled up in a corner,
Madelon came upon more than one portrait
of herself, a pale-faced, curly-headed child,
who looked out at her from the canvas with
wistful brown eyes that seemed full of the
thoughts that at that time had begun to
agitate her poor little brain. How the sight
of them brought back the old vanished days !
How it stirred within her sudden tender
recollections of the quiet hours when,
dressed out in some quaint head-gear, or con-
tadina costume, or merely in her own every-

day frock, she had sat perched up on a high stool, or on a pile of boxes, dreaming to herself, or listening to the talk between the two men.

"That man is a fool," the American would exclaim, dashing his brush across a whole morning's work; "that man is a presumptuous fool who, here in Florence, here where those others have lived and died, dares to stand before an easel and imagine that he can paint—and I have been that man!" He was wont to grow noisy and loquacious over his failures—not moody and dumb, as some men do.

"You concern yourself too much," M. Linders would reply calmly, putting the finishing touch to Madelon as a *bergère* standing in the midst of a flock of sheep, and a green landscape—like the enlarged top of a *bonbonnière*. "You are too ambitious, *mon cher*—you are little, and want to be great—

hence your discomfort; whilst I, who am little, and know it, remain content."

" May I be spared such content !" growled the other, who was daily exasperated by the atrocities his friend produced by way of pictures. It was beyond his comprehension how any man could paint such to his disgrace, and then calmly contemplate them as the work of his own hands. " Heaven preserve me from such content, I say !"

" But it is there you are all in the wrong," says M. Linders, quite unmoved by his companion's uncomplimentary energy. " You agitate, you disturb yourself with the idea that some day you will become something great—you begin to compare yourself with these men whose works you are for ever copying, with who knows ?—with Raffaelle, with Da Vinci——"

" I compare myself with them !" cries the American, interrupting him. " I ! No, *mon*

ami, I am not quite such a fool as that. I
reverence them, I adore their memory, I
bow down before their wonderful genius "—
and as he spoke he lifted his cap from his
head, suiting his action to his words—" but
compare myself!—I !" Then picking up his
brush again, he added, " But the world
needs its little men as well as its great ones
—at any rate, the little ones need their *pot
au feu ;* so to work again. *Allons, ma petite,*
your head a little more this way."

This little conversation, which occurred
nearly at the beginning of their acquaintance,
the painter's words and manner, his energy,
his simple, dignified gesture as he raised his
cap—all made a great impression on our
Madelon ; it was indeed one of her first
lessons in that hero-worship whereby lesser
minds are brought into *rapport* with great
ones ; and, even while they reverence afar
off, exultingly feel that they in some sort

share in their genius through their power of appreciating it. Nor was it her last lesson of the same kind.

Her second friend was an old German violinist, who inhabited two little rooms at the top of the big house, a tall, broadshouldered, stooping man, whose thick yellow hair and moustache, plentifully mixed with grey, blue eyes, and fair complexion, testified to his nationality, as did his queer, uncouth accent, though he had spent at least two-thirds of his life in Florence. He was an old friend of the American painter's, and paid frequent visits to his studio; and it was there he first met Madelon and her father. He did not much affect M. Linders' company, but he took a fancy to the child, as indeed most people did, and made her promise that she would come and see him; and when she had once found her way, and been welcomed to his little bare room,

where an old piano, a violin, and heaps of
dusty folios of music, were the principal furniture, a day seldom passed without her
paying him a visit. She would perch herself at his window, which commanded a
wide view over the city, with its countless
roofs, and domes, and towers, and beyond
the encircling hills, with their scattered
villas, and slopes of terraced gardens, and
pines, and olives, all under the soft blue
transparent sky; and with her eyes fixed
on this sunny view, Madelon would go off
into some dreamy fit, as she listened to the
violinist, of whose playing she never wearied.
He was devoted to his art, though he had
never attained to any remarkable proficiency
in it; and at any hour of the day he might
be heard scraping, and tuning, and practising,
for he belonged to the orchestra of one of
the theatres. It was quite a new sensation
for Madelon to hear so much music in private

life, and she thought it all beautiful—tuning
and scraping and all.

"But that is all rubbish," the German
would cry, after spending an hour in going
through some trashy modern Italian music.
"Now, my child, you shall hear something
worth listening to;" and with a sigh of relief
he would turn to some old piece by Mozart
or Bach, some minuet of Haydn's, some romance of Beethoven's, which he would play
with no great power of execution, indeed,
but with a rare sweetness and delicacy of
touch and expression, and with an intense
absorption in the music, which communicated itself to even so small a listener as
Madelon.

It would have been hard to say which of
the two had the more enjoyment—she, as
she sat motionless, her chin propped on her
two hands, her brown eyes gazing into
space, and a hundred dreamy fancies vague-

ly shaped by the music, flitting through her
brain; or he, as he bent over his violin,
lovingly extracting the sweet sounds, and
his thoughts—who knows where?—anywhere, one may be sure, rather than in the
low-ceiled, dusty garret, redolent of to-
bacco smoke, and not altogether free from
a suspicion of onions.

"There, my child," he would say at the
end, " that is music—that is art! What I
was playing before was mere rubbish—
trash, unworthy of me and of my violin."

"And why do you play it?" asks Madelon, simply.

"Ah! why, indeed?" said the violinist—
"because one must live, my little Fräulein;
and since they will play nothing else at the
theatre, I must play it also, or I should be
badly off."

"You are not rich, then?" said Madelon.

"Rich enough," he answered. " I gain

enough to live upon, and I ask no more."

"Why don't you make money like papa?" says Madelon; "then you could play what you liked, you know. We are very rich sometimes."

The old German screwed up his queer, kind, ugly face.

"It—it's not my way," he said drily. "As for money, I might have had plenty by this time, if I had not run away from home when I was a boy, because I preferred being a poor musician to a rich merchant. Money is not the only nor the best thing in the world, my little lady."

M. Linders apparently saw no danger to Madelon's principles in these new friend-ships, or else, perhaps, he was bent on carrying out his plan of letting her get used to things; at any rate, he did not interfere with her spending as much time as she liked with both painter and musician; and

every day through the winter she grew
fonder of the society of the old violinist.
He was a lonely man, who lived with his
music and his books, cared little for company, and had few friends; but he liked to
see Madelon flitting about his dusky room,
carrying with her bright suggestions of the
youth, and gaiety, and hopefulness he had
almost forgotten. He talked to her, taught
her songs, played to her as much as she
liked, and often gave her and her father
orders for the theatre to which he belonged,
where, with delight, she would recognise his
familiar face as he nodded and smiled at
her from the orchestra. He instructed her,
too, in music; made her learn her notes,
and practise on the jangling old piano, and
even, at her particular request, to scrape a
little on the violin; but she cared most for
singing, and for hearing him play and talk.
She never felt shy or timid with him, and

one day, at the end of a long rhapsody
about German music and German com-
posers, she asked him innocently enough—

"Who was Beethoven, and Mozart, and
—and all those others you talk about? I
never heard of them before."

"Never before!" he cried, in a sort of
comic amazement and dismay. "Here is a
little girl who has lived half her life in Germany, who talks German, and yet never
heard of Beethoven, nor of Mozart, nor of
—of all those others! Listen, then—they
were some of the greatest men that ever
lived."

And, indeed, Madelon heard enough about
them after that; for delighted to have a
small, patient listener, to whom he could
rhapsodize as much as he pleased in his
native tongue, the violinist henceforth lost
no opportunity of delivering his little lec-
tures, and would harangue for an hour to-

gether, not only about music and musicians, but about a thousand other things —a queer, high-flown, rambling jumble, often enough, which Madelon could not possibly follow nor understand, but to which she nevertheless liked to listen. A safer teacher she could hardly have had ; she gained much positive information from him, and when he got altogether beyond her, she remained impressed with the conviction that he was speaking from the large experiences of deep, mysterious wisdom and knowledge, and sat listening with a reverential awe, as to some strange, lofty strain, coming to her from some higher and nobler region than she could hope to attain to as yet, and of which she could in some sort catch the spirit, though she could not enter into the idea. At the same time there was a certain childlike vein running through all the old man's rambling talk, which made it, after all, not unsuited to meet the instinctive aspirations of a child's mind. With him love and veneration for greatness and beauty, in every form, amounted almost to a passion, which was still fresh and genuine, as in the lad to whom the realization of the word *blasé* seems the one incomprehensible impossibility of life. In the simple reverence with which he spoke of the great masters of his art, Madelon might have recognized the same spirit as that which animated the American ; and as the artist had once uncovered at the name of Raffaelle and Lionardo da Vinci, so did the musician figuratively bow down at the shrines of Handel, or Bach, or Beethoven. From both these men, so different in other respects, the child began to learn the same lesson, which in all her life before she had never even heard hinted at.

All this, however, almost overtaxed our little Madelon's faculties, and it was not sur-

prising that, as the winter wore on, a change
gradually came over her. In truth, both
intellect and imagination were being over-
strained by the constant succession of new
images, new ideas, new thoughts, that presented themselves to her. She by no means
grew accustomed to churches—not in the
sense, at any rate, which her father had
hoped would be the result of his new system.
It was not possible that she should, while so
much remained that was mysterious and un-
explained; she only wearied her small brain
with the effort to find the explanation for
all these new perplexities, which she felt
must exist somewhere, though she could
not find it; add to this, these long conversa-
tions, this music, with its strange, vague
suggestions, and even the thousand novel-
ties of the picturesque Italian life around
her, not one of which was lost on her im-

pressionable little mind, and we need not
wonder that she began to suffer from an
excitement that gathered in strength from
day to day. She grew thin, morbid, nervous,
ate almost nothing, and lost her usual vi-
vacity, sitting absorbed in dreamy fits, from
which it was difficult to arouse her, and
which were very different from the quiet,
happy silence in which she used to remain
contented by her father's side for hours.
All night she was haunted with what she
had seen by day in picture-galleries and
churches. The heavenly creations of Fra
Angelico or Sandro Botticelli, of Ghirlan-
daio or Raffaelle, over which she had mused
and pondered, re-produced themselves in
dreams, with the intensity and reality of
actual visions, and with accessories borrowed
from all that, in her new life, had impressed
itself most vividly on her imagination. Once

N 2

more she would stand in the vast church, the censers swinging, the organ pealing overhead, round her a great throng of beatified adoring saints, with golden glories, with palms, and tall white lilies, and many-coloured garments; or pillars and arches would melt away, and she would find herself wandering through flower-enamelled grass, in fair rose-gardens of Paradise; or radiant forms would come gliding towards her through dark-blue skies; or the heavens themselves would seem to open, and reveal a blaze of glory, where, round a blue-robed, star-crowned Madonna, choirs of rapturous angels repeated the divine melodies she had heard faintly echoed in the violinist's dim little room. All day long these dreams clung to her, oppressing her with their strange unreal semblance of reality, associating themselves with every glowing sunset, with every starry sky, till the pictures themselves that had suggested them looked pale by comparison.

She was, in fact, going through a mental crisis, such as, in other circumstances, and under fostering influences, has produced more than one small ecstatic enthusiast; the infant shining light of some Methodist conventicle; the saintly child visionary of some Catholic convent. But Madelon had no one to foster, nor to interpret for her these feverish visions, so inexplicable to herself, poor child! To the good-natured, careless, jovial American, she would not have even hinted at them for worlds, and not less carefully did she shun appealing to her father for sympathy. That contemptuous "*vraiment*" dwelt in her memory, not as a matter of resentment, but as something to be avoided henceforth at the cost of any amount of self-repression. She would sit leaning her languid little head on his

shoulder; but when he anxiously asked her
what ailed her, she could only reply, " I
don't know, papa." And indeed she did
not know; nor even if she had, could she
have found the words with which to have
explained it to him. It was, after all, the
old German who won her confidence at last.
There was, as we have said, something
simple, genuine, homely about the old man;
a reminiscence, perhaps, of his homely
Fatherland still clinging about him, after
more than forty years of voluntary exile,
which Madelon could well appreciate, though
she could not have defined it; for a child
judges more by instinct than reflection, and
it was through no long process of reasoning
that she had arrived at the certainty that
she would be met here by neither contempt
nor indifference. Moreover, his generally
lofty and slightly incomprehensible style of

conversation, and the endless stores of
learning with which she had innocently ac-
credited him, had surrounded him with that
vague halo of wisdom and goodness, so dear
to the hearts of children of larger as of
smaller growth, and which they are so eager
to recognize, that they do not always distin-
guish between the false and the true. From
the very beginning of their acquaintance, it
had occurred to Madelon that she might be
able to gain some information on that subject, which her father had pronounced to be
above her comprehension as yet ; but which,
on reflection, and encouraged by a Nanette's
example, she felt quite sure she could
understand if it were only explained to her.
Twenty times had that still unanswered
question trembled on her lips, but a shy
timidity, not so much of her old friend as of
the subject itself, which had become invested

in her mind with a kind of awful mystery, to which a hundred circumstances daily contributed, checked her at the moment of utterance.

One evening, however, she was sitting as usual at the window in the old man's room. The sun had set, the short twilight was drawing to a close, church bells were ringing, down in the city yellow lights were gleaming in windows here and there, above, the great sky rounded upwards from a faint glow on the horizon through imperceptible gradations of tint, to pure depths of transparent blue overhead, where stars were beginning to flash and tremble; within, in the gloom, the musician sat playing a sacred melody of Spohr's, and as Madelon listened, some subtle affinity between this hour and the first one she had spent in the church touched her, and her eyes filled with sudden tears of painful ecstasy. As the old German ceased, she went up to him with an impulse that admitted of no hesitation, and, as well as she could, told him all that was in her mind— her dreams, her strange weird fancies, all that for the last few months had been haunting and oppressing her with its weight of mystery. " Papa said I could not understand," she said in conclusion, " but I think I could. Will you not explain it to me? Can you not tell me what it all means, and who—who is God ?"

The German had heard in silence till then, but at this last question he started from his listening attitude.

" *Was—was—*" he stammered, and suddenly rising—"*Ach, mein Gott !*" he cried, with the familiar ejaculation, " to ask me !— to ask me !"

He walked twice up and down the room, as stirred by some hidden emotion, his head bowed, his hands behind his back, murmur-

ing to himself, and then stopped where
Madelon was standing by the window. She
looked up, half trembling, into the rugged
face bent over her. He was her priest for
the moment, standing as it were between
earth and heaven—her confessor, to whom
she had revealed the poor little secrets of
her heart; and she waited with a sort of
awe for his answer.

"My child," he said at length, looking
down sadly enough into her eager, inquiring
eyes, "when I was no older than thou art,
I had a pious, gentle mother, at whose
knee night and morning I said my prayers—
and believed. If she were alive now, I
would say, 'Go to her, and she will tell
thee of all these things'—but do not speak
of them to me. Old Karl Wendler is neither
good, nor wise, nor believing enough to
instruct thee, an innocent child."

He made this little speech very gently and solemnly; then turned away abruptly, took up his hat, and left the room without another word. Madelon stood still for a minute, baffled, repulsed, with a sort of bruised, sore feeling at her heart, and yet with a new sense of wondering pity, roused by something in his words and manner; then she too left the room, and through the darkness crept softly downstairs.

So ended this little episode with the violinist. Not that she did not visit and sit with him as much as before; the very next day, when she returned, rather shyly, upstairs, she found him sitting in the old place, with the old nod and smile to welcome her, but somehow he managed to put things on a different footing—he spared her his long metaphysical discourses, and talked to her more as the child that she was,

laughing, joking, and telling her queer hob-
goblin and fairy stories, some of which she
knew before indeed, but which he related
with a quaint simplicity and naïveté, which
gave them a fresh charm for her; and under
this new aspect of things, she brightened
up, began to lose her fits of dreaminess, to
chatter as in old times, and cheered many
an hour of the musician's solitary life. The
American artist, too, left Florence about
this time for a visit to Rome; and during his
absence the *atelier* was closed, and wanderings through churches and picture galleries
were exchanged for long excursions into the
country with her father; by degrees dreams,
fancies, visions floated away, and Madelon
became herself again.

She had gone through a phase, and one
not altogether natural to her, and which
readily passed away with the abnormal con-

ditions that had occasioned it. She was by
no means one of those dreamy, thoughtful,
often melancholy children who startle us by
the precocious grasp of their intellect, by
their intuitive perception of truths which
we had deemed far above their comprehension. Madelon's precocity was of quite
another order. In her quick, impulsive,
energetic little mind there was much that
was sensitive and excitable, little that was
morbid or unhealthy. One might see that,
with her, action would always willingly take
the place of reflection; that her impulses
would have the strength of inspirations;
that she would be more ready to receive
impressions than to reason upon them.
Meditation, comparison, introspection, were
wholly foreign to this little, eager, impetu-
ous nature, however they might be forced
upon it in the course of years and events;

and with her keen sense of enjoyment in all
glad outward influences, one might have
feared that the realities of life present to
her would too readily preclude any con-
templation of its hidden possibilities, but
for a lively, susceptible imagination, which
would surely intervene to prevent any such
tendency being carried out to its too pro-
saic end. It was through appeals to her
imagination and affection, rather than to her
reason and intellect, that Madeleine could be
influenced; and whatever large sympathies
with humanity she might acquire through
life, whatever aspirations after a high and
noble ideal, whatever gleams of inspiration
from the great beyond that lies below the
widest, as well as the narrowest horizon,
might visit her—all these would come to
her, we may fancy, through the exercise of
pure instincts and a sensitive imagination,

rather than through the power of logical deduction from given causes.

From our small, ten-year-old Madelon, however, all this still lay hidden; for the present, the outward pressure, which had weighed too heavily on her little mind and brain, removed, she returned with a glad reaction to her old habits of thought and speech. Not entirely, indeed; the education she had received, remained and worked; the "obstinate questionings," an answer to which she had twice vainly sought, were unforgotten, and still awaited their reply. This little Madelon, to whom the golden gates had been opened, though ever so slightly—to whom the divine, lying all about her and within her, had been revealed, though ever so dimly—could never be quite the same as the little Madelon who, careless and unthinking, had strayed into the great church that summer morning six months ago; but the child herself was as yet hardly conscious of this, and neither, we may be sure, was M. Linders, as with renewed cheerfulness, and spirits, and chatter, she danced along by his side under the new budding trees, under the fair blue skies.

It was soon after this, when the delicious promise of an early spring was brightening the streets and gardens of Florence, filling them with sunshine and flowers, that another shadow fell upon the brightness of Madelon's life, and one so dark and real, as to make all others seem faint and illusory by comparison. Her father had a serious illness. He had not been well all the winter; and one day, Madelon, coming down from the violinist's room, had been frightened almost out of her small wits at finding him lying back unconscious in a chair in

their little *salon*. She called the old woman who acted as their servant to her assistance, and between them they had soon
succeeded in restoring him to consciousness,
when he had made light of it, saying it was
merely a fit of giddiness, which would have
passed off. He had refused to be alarmed,
or to send for a doctor, even after a second
and third attack of the same kind; but then
a fever, which in the mild spring weather
was lurking about, lying in wait for victims,
seized him, and laid him fairly prostrate.

His illness never took a really dangerous
turn, but it kept him weak and helpless for
some weary weeks, during which Madelon
learnt to be a most efficient little nurse,
taking turns with the old servant and with
the violinist, who willingly came down from
his upper regions to do all he could to help
his little favourite. In some respects she,
perhaps, made the best nurse of all, with

her small skilful fingers, and entire devotion
to her father.   She had a curious courage,
too, for such an inexperienced child, and
the sense of an emergency was quite sufficient to make her conquer the horrible
pang it gave her loving little heart to see
her father lying racked with pain, unconscious, and sometimes delirious.   She never
failed to be ready when wanted ; the doctor
complimented her, and said jokingly · that
the little Signorina would make a capital
doctor's assistant.   Her German friend
nodded approval, and, best of all, it was
always to his Madelon that M. Linders
turned in his most weary moments—from
her that he liked to receive drinks and me-
dicine ; and she it was who, as he declared,
arranged his pillows and coverings more
comfortably than anyone else.   In delirium
he asked for her continually ; his eyes sought

her when she was not in the room, and lighted up when she came with her little noiseless step to his bedside. The old German, who had had a strong dislike to, and prejudice against this man, took almost a liking for him, as he noted the great love existing between him and his little daughter.

The American did not return till M. Linders was nearly well again, and thinking of departure. Madelon was in despair at the idea of leaving Florence; it had been more like home to her than any place she had yet known, and it almost broke her heart to think of parting with her old German friend; but M. Linders was impatient to be gone. He wanted change of air, he said, after his illness; but, indeed, had other reasons which he proclaimed less openly, but which were far more imperative,

and made him anxious to pay an earlier
visit to Germany this year than was usual
with him.   Certain speculations, on the
success of which he had counted, had failed,
so that a grand *coup* at Homburg or Baden
seemed no less necessary than desirable to
set him straight again with the world, and
he accordingly fixed on a day towards the
end of April for their departure.

The American made a festive little supper the evening before in his *atelier*, but it
was generally felt to be a melancholy failure, for not even the artist's rather forced
gaiety, nor M. Linders' real indifference,
could enliven it.   As for the old German,
he sat there, saying little, eating less, and
smoking a great deal; and Madelon at his
side was speechless, only rousing herself
later in the evening to coax him into playing once more all her favourite tunes.
Everyone, except, perhaps, M. Linders, felt

more or less sorry at the breaking up of a pleasant little society which had lasted for some months, and the violinist almost felt as if he were being separated from his own child. Madelon wished him good-bye that night, but she ran upstairs very early the next morning to see him once more before starting.

The old man was greatly moved; he was standing looking sadly out of the window when she came in, and when he saw her in her little travelling cloak, the tears began to run down his rugged old cheeks.

"God bless thee, my little one!" he said. "I shall miss thee sorely—but thou wilt not forget me?"

"Never, never!" cries Madelon, with a little sob, and squeezing the kind hands that held hers so tightly.

"And if I should never see thee again,"

said the German, in broken accents, " if—if
—remember, I——" He hesitated and
stammered, and M. Linders' voice was heard
calling Madelon.

" I must go," she said, "papa is calling
me ; but I will never forget you—never;
ah! you have been so good, so kind to me.
See here," she said, unclosing one of her
hands which she had kept tightly shut, and
showing the little green and gold fish
Horace Graham had given her years before,
" I promised never to part with this, but I
have nothing else—and—and I love you
so much—will you have it ?"

" No, no," said the old man, smiling and
shaking his head, "keep thy promise and
thy treasure, my child ; I do not require
that to remind me of thee.   Farewell!"

He put her gently out of the door as her
father's step was heard coming upstairs, and

closed it after her. She never did see him again, for he died in less than two years after their parting.

M. Linders went to Homburg, to Baden, to Wiesbaden, but he was no longer the man he had been before his illness; he won largely, indeed, at times, but he lost as largely at others, playing with a sort of reckless, feverish impatience, instead of with the steady coolness that had distinguished him formerly. Old acquaintance who met him said that M. Linders was a broken man, and that his best days were over; men who had been accustomed to bet on his success, shrugged their shoulders, and sought for some steadier and luckier player to back; he himself, impatient of ill-luck, and of continual defeat in the scenes of his former triumphs, grew restless and irritable, wandered from place to place in search of better fortune and better health, and at length, at the end of a fortnight's stay at Wiesbaden, after winning a large sum at *rouge-et-noir*, and losing half of it the next day, announced abruptly that he was tired of Germany, and should set off at once for Paris. Madelon had noticed the alteration in her father less than anyone else perhaps; she was used to changes of fortune, and whatever he might feel he never showed it in his manner to her; outwardly, at least, this summer had appeared to her very similiar to any preceding one, and she was too much accustomed to M. Linders' sudden moves, to find anything unusual in this one, although, dictated as it was by a caprice of weariness and disgust, it took them away from the German tables just at the height of the season. Once more, then, the two set out together, and towards the

middle of August found themselves established in their old quarters in the Paris
Hotel, where Madame Linders had died,
and where Madame Lavaux still reigned
head of the establishment.

PART II.

CHAPTER I.

AFTER FIVE YEARS.

ONE evening, about three weeks after their arrival in Paris, Madelon was standing at a window at the end of the long corridor into which M. Linders' apartment opened ; the moon was shining brightly, and she had a book in her hand, which she was reading by its clear light, stopping, however, every minute to gaze down into the front courtyard of the hotel, which lay beneath the window, quiet, almost deserted after the bustle of the day, and full of white moon-light and black shadows. Her father was out, and she was watching for his return, though it was now long past eleven o'clock.

There was nothing unusual on her part in this late vigil, for she was quite accustomed to sit up for her father, when he spent his evenings away from home; but there must have been something strange and forlorn-looking in the little figure standing there all alone at such an hour, for a gentleman, who had come in late from the theatre, paused as he was turning the key of the door before entering his room, looked at her once or twice, and, after a moment's hesitation, walked up to the window. Madelon did not notice him till he was close behind her, and then turned round with a little start, dropping her book.

" I did not think it was you—" she began ; then seeing a stranger, stopped short in the middle of her speech.

"I am afraid I have startled you," said

the gentleman in English-French, but with a pleasant voice and manner, " and disappointed you too."

" I beg your pardon, Monsieur," she answered, " I thought it was papa ; I have been looking for him for so long," and she turned round to the window again.

It was five years since Horace Graham and Madeleine had spent an hour together in the courtyard at Chaudfontaine, so that it was not surprising that they did not at once recognise each other at this second unforeseen meeting; the young man, as well as the child, had then been of an age to which five years cannot be added without bringing with them most appreciable changes. For Graham, these years had been precisely that transition period in which a lad separates himself from the aggregate mass of youth, and stands forth in the world as a man in his own right, according to that which is in him.

This tall, thin, brown young army doctor, who has passed brilliant examinations, who is already beginning to be known favourably in the profession, whose name has appeared at the end of more than one approved article in scientific Reviews; who has travelled, seen something of Italy, Switzerland, Belgium; who for five years has been studying, thinking, living through youthful experiences and failures, and out-living some youthful illusions, cannot fail, one may be sure, to be a different personage, in many respects, from the fresh-hearted medical student who had sauntered away an idle Sunday amongst the woods and valleys round Chaudfontaine, and had looked with curious, half wondering eyes at the new little world disclosed to him at the hotel. As for our little Madelon, the small, round, pinafored child was hardly recognisable in this slim little girl, in a white frock, with brown hair that hung in short wayward tangling waves, instead of curling in soft ringlets all over her head; and yet Graham, who rarely forgot a face, was haunted by a vague remembrance of her eyes, with the peculiar look, half-startled, half-confiding, with which they met the first glance of strangers. Madelon's brown eyes were the greatest charm of a face which was hardly pretty yet, though it had the promise of beauty in after years; to liken them to those of some dumb, soft, dark-eyed animal is to use a trite comparison; and yet there is, perhaps, no other that so well describes eyes such as these, which seem charged with a meaning beyond that with which their owner is able to express in words, or is, perhaps, even conscious of. When seen in children, they seem to contain a whole prophecy of their future lives, and in Madelon they had probably a large share in the powers of attraction which she un-

doubtedly possessed; few could resist their
mute appeal, which, child as she was, went
beyond her own thought, and touched deep-
er sympathies than any she could yet have
known.

There was a moment's silence after Madelon had spoken, and then she once more
turned from the window with a disappointed
air.

" Pardon, Monsieur," she said again,
"but can you tell me what time it is?   Is it
past eleven?"

" It is more than half-past," said Graham, looking at his watch, "Have you been
waiting here long?"

" Since ten o'clock," said Madelon, "papa
said he would be in by ten.   I cannot think
where he can be."

" He has probably found something to de-
tain him," suggested Graham.

" No," answered Madelon, rejecting this

obvious proposition; "for he had an appointment here; there is some one waiting for him now."

"Then he has perhaps come in without your knowing it?"

"I do not think so," said Madelon, "he would have called me; and besides, I should have seen him cross the courtyard. I saw you come in just now, Monsieur."

Nevertheless she left her station by the window, and moved slowly along the passage to their apartment; it was just opposite Graham's, and as she went in, leaving the door open, Horace, who had followed her without any very definite purpose, looked in. It was a tolerably large room, with a door to the left opening into a smaller apartment, Utrecht velvet chairs and sofa, a mantelpiece also covered with velvet, on which stood a clock, a tall looking-glass, and two lighted wax candles; a table in the middle with some packs of cards, and a liqueur bottle and glasses, and a bed on one side opposite the fireplace. The window looked on to a side street, noisy with the incessant rattling of vehicles, and so narrow that the numerous lighted interiors of the houses opposite were visible to the most casual observer. A smell of smoking pervaded the room, explained by the presence of a young man, who held a cigar in one hand, whilst he leaned half out of the window, over the low iron balcony in front, shouting to some one in the street below. He looked round as Madelon came in, and slowly drew himself back into the room, exhibiting a lean, yellow face, surrounded with dishevelled hair, and ornamented by black unkempt beard and moustache.

" *Monsieur votre père* does not arrive apparently, Mademoiselle," he said.

" I have not seen him come in, Monsieur,"
answered Madelon ; " I thought he was perhaps here."

"Not at all, I have seen nothing of him
this evening. But this is perhaps a trick that
Monsieur le Papa is playing me ; he fears to
give me his little revenge of which he spoke,
and wishes to keep out of my way. What
do you say to that, Mademoiselle ?"

" I am quite sure it is not so," answered
Madelon, with a little defiant air. " I heard
papa say it was quite by chance he had lost
all that money to you, for you did not
understand the first principles of the
game."

" Ah ! he said that ? But it is lucky for
us other poor devils that we have these
chances sometimes ! You will at least admit
that, Mademoiselle ?"

"Papa plays better than anyone," says
Madelon, retreating from argument to the

safer ground of assertion, and still standing in the middle of the room in her defiant attitude, with her hands clasped behind her.

" Without a doubt, Mademoiselle; but then, as he says, we also have our chances. Well, I cannot wait for mine this evening, for it is nearly midnight, and I have another appointment. These gentlemen will wonder what has become of me. Mademoiselle, I have the honour to wish you good evening."

He made a profound bow, and left the room.

Madelon gave a great sigh, and then came out into the passage again where Horace was standing. He had been a somewhat bewildered spectator of this queer little interview, but the child evidently saw nothing out of the way in it, for she made no remark upon it, and only said rather piteously,

" I cannot imagine where papa can be; I do wish he would come back."

"Does he often stay out so late as this?" asked Graham.

"Oh! yes, often, but not when he says he is coming in early, or when he is expecting anyone."

"And do you know where he is gone?"

"No, not at all. He said he was going to dine with some gentlemen, but I don't know where. Oh! do you think anything —anything can have happened?" cried Madelon, her hidden anxiety suddenly finding utterance.

"Indeed I do not," answered Graham, in his kindest voice. "His friends have persuaded him to stay late, I have no doubt; you must not be so uneasy—these things often happen, you know. Let us go and look out of the window again; perhaps we shall see him just coming in."

They went to the end of the corridor accordingly; but no one was to be seen, except

the man who had just left M. Linders' apartment walking briskly across the moonlit
space below, the great doors of the *porte-
cochère* closing after him with a clang that
resounded through the silent courtyard.
Graham had nothing further to say in the
way of consolation; he could think of no
more possible contingencies to suggest, and,
indeed, it was useless to go on reasoning
concerning perfectly unknown conditions.
Madelon, however, seemed a little reassured
by his confident tone, and he changed the
subject by asking her whether the gentleman
who had just left was a friend of hers.

"Who? Monsieur Legros?" Madelon answered. "No, I don't know him much, and
I do not like him at all; he comes sometimes to play with papa."

"To play with him?"

"Yes, at cards, you know—at *écarté*, or
piquet, or one of those games."

" And it was with him that your father had an appointment ?"

" Yes," said Madelon; " he came last night, and papa told him to be here again this evening at ten, and that is why I cannot think why he does not come."

She turned again disconsolately to the window, and there was another pause. Madelon relapsed into the silence habitual to her with strangers, and Graham hardly knew how to continue the conversation; yet he was unwilling to leave the child alone with her anxiety at that late hour; and besides, he was haunted by vague, floating memories that refused to shape themselves definitely. Some time—somewhere—he had heard or seen, or dreamt of some one—he could not catch the connecting link which would serve to unite some remote, foregone experience with his present sensations.

He moved a little away from the window,

and in so doing his foot struck against the book which Madelon had dropped on first seeing him, and he stooped to pick it up. It was a German story-book, full of bright coloured pictures; so he saw as he opened it and turned over the leaves, scarcely thinking of what he did, when his eye was suddenly arrested by the inscription on the fly-leaf. The book had been given to Madelon only the year before by a German lady she had met at Chaudfontaine, and there was her name, "Madeleine Linders," that of the donor, the date, and below, "Hôtel des Bains, Chaudfontaine." It was a revelation to Horace. Of course he understood it all now. Here was the clue to his confused recollections, to the strange little scene he had just witnessed. Another moonlit courtyard came to his remembrance, a gleaming, rushing river, a background of shadowy hills, and a little coy, wilful, chattering girl, with curly

hair and great brown eyes—those very eyes
that had been perplexing him not ten minutes
ago.

" I think you and I have met before," he
said to Madelon, smiling; " but I daresay
you don't remember much about it, though
I recollect you very well now."

" We have met before?" said Madelon.
" Pardon, Monsieur, but I do not very well
recall it."

" At Chaudfontaine, five years ago, when
you were quite a little girl. You are Madeleine Linders, are you not?"

" Yes, I am Madeleine Linders," she answered. " I have often been to Chaudfontaine; did you stay at the hotel there?"

" Only for one night," said Graham; " but
you and I had a long talk together in the
courtyard that evening. Let me see, how
can I recall it to you? Ah! there was a
little green and gold fish——"

" Was that you ?" cried Madelon, her face
suddenly brightening with a flush of intelligence and pleasure. "I have it still, that
little fish. Ah ! how glad I am now that I
did not give it away! That gentleman was
so kind to me, I shall never forget him.
But it was you !" she added, with a sudden
recognition of Graham's identity.

"It was indeed," he said laughing. "So
you have thought of me sometimes since
then ? But I am afraid you would not
have remembered me if I had not told you
who I was."

"I was such a little girl then," said Madelon colouring. "Five years ago—why I was
not six years old ; but I remember you
very well now," she added, smiling up
at him. "I have often thought of you,
Monsieur, and I am so glad to see you
again."

She said it with a little naïve air of frank-

ness and sincerity which was very engaging,
giving him her hand as she spoke.

"I am glad you have not quite forgotten
me," said Graham, sitting down by her on
the window seat; "but indeed you have
grown so much, I am not sure I should
have recollected you, if I had not seen your
name here. What have you been doing
ever since? Have you ever been to Chaudfontaine again?"

"Oh, very often," said Madelon. "We
go there almost every year for a little
while—not this year though, for we were at
Wiesbaden till three weeks ago, and then
papa had to come to Paris at once."

"And do you still go about everywhere
with your papa, or do you go to school
sometimes?"

"To school? oh no, never," said Madelon,
not without some wonder at the idea.
"Papa would not send me to school. I

should not like it at all, and neither would
he.   I know he would not get on at all
well without me, and I love travelling about
with him.   Last winter we were in Italy."

" And you never come to England ?"

" No, never.   I asked papa once if he
would not go there, and he said no, that
we should not like it at all, it was so cold
and *triste* there, one never amused one's-
self."

" But I thought you had some relations
there," said Graham.   " Surely I saw an
uncle with you who was English ?"

"Oh yes, Uncle Charles; but he never
went to England either, and he died a long
time ago.   I don't know of any other relations."

" So you never talk English now, I suppose?   Do you remember telling me to
speak English, because I spoke French so
funnily ?"

"No," said Madelon, colouring and laughing. "How is it possible I can have been so rude, Monsieur? I think you speak it very well. But I have not forgotten my English, for I have some books, and often we meet English or American gentlemen, so that I still talk it sometimes."

"And German too," said Horace, looking at her book.

"Yes, and Italian; I learnt that last winter at Florence. We meet a great many different people, you know, so I don't forget."

"And you are always travelling about?"

"Yes, always; I should not like to live in one place, I think, and papa would not like it either, he says. Do you remember papa, Monsieur?"

"Very well," said Graham; and indeed he recalled perfectly the little scene in the salle-à-manger of the Chaudfontaine hotel

—the long dimly lighted room, the two men playing at cards, and the little child nestling close up to the fair one whom she called papa. "Yes, I remember him very well," he added, after a moment's pause.

"How strange that you should see us here again!" said Madelon. "Did you know we were staying in the hotel, Monsieur?"

"Not at all," answered Horace, smiling. "I only arrived yesterday, and had no notion that I should find an old acquaintance to welcome me."

"How fortunate that I was waiting here, and that you saw my name in that book," said Madelon, evidently looking on the whole as a great event, brought about by a more remarkable combination of circumstances than everyday life as a rule afforded. "Without that you would not have known who I was, perhaps? Papa will be very glad to see you again. Ah, how I wish he would come!" she added, all her anxieties suddenly revived.

"Do you always sit up for him when he is so late?" said Graham. "Surely it would be wiser for you to go to bed."

"That is just what I said to Mademoiselle an hour ago," said a kind, cheery voice behind them, belonging to Madame Lavaux, the mistress of the hotel. "Of what use, I say, is it for her to sit up waiting for her papa, who will not come any the sooner for that."

"Ah! Madame, I must wait," said Madelon. "Papa will come soon."

"But, *ma chère petite*—" began Madame.

"I must wait," repeated Madelon, piteously; "I always sit up for him."

Graham thought he could not do better than leave her in the hands of the landlady, and with a friendly good-night, and a pro-

mise to come and see her the next day, he
went back to his own room. In a few
minutes, he heard Madame pass along the
corridor and go upstairs to bed; but, though
tired enough himself after a day of Paris
sight-seeing, he could not make up his mind
to do the same, when, on opening his door,
he saw Madeleine standing.where he had
left her. He could not get rid of the
thought of this lonely little watcher at the
end of the passage, and taking up a book he
began to read. From time to time he looked out, but there was no change in the pos-
ture of affairs; through the half-open door
opposite he could see the lights burning in
the still empty room, and the small figure
remained motionless at the moonlit window.
All sounds of life and movement were hushed
in the hotel, all the clocks had long since
struck midnight, and he was considering
whether he should not go and speak to

Madelon again, when he heard a faint cry, and then a rush of light feet along the passage and down the staircase.

"So he has come at last," thought Graham, laying down his book with a sense of relief, not sorry to have his self-imposed vigil brought to an end. He still sat listening, however; his door was ajar, and he thought he should hear the father and child come up together. There was a moment's silence as the sound of the footsteps died away, and then succeeded a quick opening and shutting of doors, the tread of hasty feet, a confusion of many voices speaking at once, a sudden clamour and stir breaking in on the stillness, and then suddenly subdued and hushed, as if to suit the prevailing quiet of the sleeping house.

"Something must have happened," thought Graham. "That poor child!—perhaps her father has, after all, met with some acci-

dent !" He left his room and ran quickly
downstairs. The confused murmur of voices
grew louder as he approached the hall, and
on turning the last angle of the staircase, he
at once perceived the cause of the disturbance.

A little group was collected in the middle
of the hall, the night porter, one or two
of the servants of the hotel, and some men
in blouses, all gathered round a tall prostrate man, half lying on a bench placed
under the centre lamp, half supported by
two men, who had apparently just carried
him in. He was quite insensible, his head
had fallen forward on his breast, and was
bound with a handkerchief that had been
tied round to staunch the blood from a
wound in his forehead; his neckcloth was
unfastened and his coat thrown back to give
him more air. The little crowd was increasing every moment, as the news spread

through the house; the *porte-cochère* stood wide open, and outside in the street a *fiacre* could be seen, standing in the moonlight.

"A doctor must be fetched at once," some-one was saying, just as Horace came up and recognized, not without difficulty, in the pale disfigured form before him, the handsome fair-haired M. Linders he had met at Chaud-fontaine five years before.

"I am a doctor," he said, coming for-ward. "Perhaps I can be of some use here."

No one seemed to notice him at first—a lad had already started in quest of a surgeon, and jumping into the empty *fiacre* that had brought the injured man to the hotel, was driving off; but Madelon turned round at the sound of Graham's voice, and looked up in his face with a new expression of hope in her eyes, instead of the blank, bewildered despair with which she had been gazing at

her father and the strange faces around. To
the poor child it seemed as if she had lived
through an unknown space of terror and
misery during the few minutes that had
elapsed since from the passage window she
had seen the *fiacre* stop, and, with the pre-
sentiment of evil which had been haunting
her during these last hours of suspense,
intensified to conviction, had flown downstairs only to meet her father's insensible
form as he was carried in. She was kneeling now by his side, and was chafing one of
his cold hands between her poor little trembling fingers; but when she saw Graham
standing at the edge of the circle she got
up, and went to him.

"Will you come to papa?" she said,
taking him by both hands and drawing him
forward.

"Don't be frightened," said Horace, in
his kind, cheerful voice, trying to encourage

her, for her face and lips were colourless, and she was trembling as with a sudden chill. He put one arm round her, and came forward to look at M. Linders.

"Allow me," he said; and this time his voice commanded attention, and imposed a moment's silence on the confusion of tongues. "I am a doctor, and can perhaps be of some use; but I must beg of you not to press round in this way. Can any one tell me what has happened?" he added, as he bent over M. Linders.

"It was an accident, Monsieur," said a man of the working-class, standing by, "this poor gentleman must have had some kind of fit, I think. I was crossing the Boulevards with him about ten o'clock; there were a good many carriages about, but we were going quietly enough, when suddenly I saw him stop, put his hand to his head, and fall down in the road. I had to run just then

to get safely across myself, and when I
reached the other side, I saw a great confusion, and heard that a carriage had driven
straight over him."

There was a moment's pause, and Madelon
said in a tremulous whisper, " Papa used to
have *vertiges* last winter, but he got quite
well again."

" To be sure," said Graham ; " and so we
must hope he will now. That was more
than two hours ago," he said, turning to the
man—" what have you been doing ever
since ?"

" We carried him into the nearest *café*,
Monsieur, and some proposed taking him to
a hospital, but after a time we found a letter
in his pocket addressed to this hotel, and
we thought it best to bring him here, as he
might have friends ; so we got a *fiacre*. But
it was a long way off, and we were obliged
to come very slowly."

" A hospital would perhaps have been the better plan," said Graham ; " or you should have found a doctor before moving him. However, now he must be carried upstairs without further delay. My poor child," he said, turning to Madelon, " you can do no good here—you had better go with Madame, who will take care of you ; will you not, Madame ?" he added, turning to the landlady, who, roused from her bed, had just appeared, after a hasty toilette.

" Yes, yes, she can come with me," said Madame Lavaux, who was not in the best of tempers at the disturbance ; " but I beg of you not to make more noise than you can help, Messieurs, or I shall have the whole house disturbed, and half the people leaving to-morrow."

The sad little procession moved quietly enough up the stairs, and along the corridor to M. Linders' room. Graham had gone on in

front, but Madame Lavaux had held back
Madelon when she would have pressed forward by the side of the men who were carrying her father, and she had yielded at first
in sheer bewilderment. She had passed
through more than one phase of emotion in
the course of the last ten minutes, poor child!
The first overwhelming shock and terror had
passed away, when Graham's reassuring voice
and manner had convinced her that her
father was not dead; but she had still felt
too stunned and confused to do more than
obey passively, as she watched him carefully
raised, and slowly carried from the hall.
By the time they reached the top of the
staircase, however, her natural energy began to reassert itself; and, as she saw him
disappear within the bedroom, her impatient
eagerness to be at his side again, could not
be restrained. His recent illness was still too
fresh a memory for the mere sight of his pre-

sent suffering and insensibility to have any of
the terrors of novelty, after the first shock was
over, and all her former experiences went
to prove that his first words on recovering
consciousness would be to ask for her. Her
one idea was that she must go at once and
nurse him; she had not heeded, nor, perhaps,
even heard Graham's last words, and she was
about to follow the men into the bedroom,
when Madame Lavaux interposed to prevent
her.

"Run upstairs to my room, *petite*," she
said; "you will be out of the way there, and
I will come to you presently."

"No," said Madelon, refusing point-blank,
"I am going with papa."

"But it is not possible, my child; you will
only be in the way. You heard what M. le
Docteur said?"

"I *will* go to papa!" cries Madelon, trembling with agitation and excitement; "he will

want me, I know he will, I am never in his
way ! You have no right to prevent my going
to him, Madame! Let me pass, I say," for
Madame Lavaux was standing between her
and the door of the room into which M. Linders had been carried.

"*Allons donc,* we must be reasonable,"
says Madame. " Your papa does not want
you now, and little girls should do as they
are told. If you had gone to bed an hour
ago, as I advised, you would have known
nothing about all this till to-morrow. Eh,
these children ! there is no doing anything
with them ; and these men," she continued
with a sigh, " the noise they make with their
great boots! and precisely Madame la Comtesse, *au premier*, had an *attaque des nerfs* this
evening, and said the house was as noisy as a
barrack—but these things always happen at
unfortunate moments !"

No one answered this little speech, which,

in fact, was addressed to no one in particular. It was, perhaps, not altogether Madame Lavaux' fault that through long habit her instincts as the proprietor of a large hotel had ended by predominating so far over her instincts as a woman as always to come to hand first. The nice adjustment between the claims of conscience and the claims of self-interest, between the demands of her bills and the demands of never-satisfied, exacting travellers, alone involved a daily recurring struggle, in which the softer emotions would have been altogether out of place, we may suppose. In the present instance she considered it a hard case that her house should be turned topsy-turvy at such an untimely hour, and its general propriety endangered thereby; and Madelon's grief, which at another time would have excited her compassion, had for the moment taken the unexpected form of determined opposition,

and could only be looked upon as another
element of disturbance. Madelon herself,
however, who could hardly be expected to
regard her father's accident with a view to
those wider issues that naturally presented
themselves to Madame Lavaux, simply felt
that she was being cruelly ill-used. She had
not attended to a word of this last speech,
but nevertheless she had detected the want
of sympathy, and it by no means increased
her desire to accede to Madame's wishes.

"I *will* go to papa," she repeated, the
sense of antagonism that had come upper-
most gaining strength and vehemence from
the consciousness of the underlying grief and
sore trouble that had aroused it, "or I will
stay here if you will not let me pass;
rather than go away I will stand here all
night."

Graham had heard nothing of this little
altercation, but now coming out of the bed-

room to speak to Madame Lavaux, he found
a most determined little Madelon standing
with her hands clasped behind her, and
her back set firmly against the wall, absolutely refusing to retreat.

She sprang forward, however, as soon as
she saw him.

"I may go to papa now, may I not?" she
cried.

"Mademoiselle wants to go to her papa,"
says Madame, at the same moment, "I beg
of you, Monsieur, to tell her it is impossible, and that she had better come with me.
She asserts that her father will want her."

"That is all nonsense," said Graham
hastily; "of course she cannot come in now,"
then noticing Madelon's poor little face, al-
ternately white, and flushed with misery and
passion, he said, "Listen to me, Madelon;
you can do your father no good now. He
would not know you, my poor child, and

you would only be in the way. But I
promise you that by-and-by you shall see
him."

"By-and-by, " said   Madelon ; " how
soon ?"

"As soon as we can possibly manage it."

Nothing, perhaps, would have induced
Madelon at that moment to have given into
Madelon Lavaux' unsupported persuasions,
but she yielded at once to Horace ; indeed
her sudden passion had already died away at
the sight of his face, at the sound of the kind
voice which she had somehow begun to associate with a sense of help and protection.
She did nöt quite give up her point even
now, however.

"I need not go upstairs?" she said, with
trembling lips and tears in her eyes. "I
may go into my own room, may I not ?"

"Your room ? Which is that ?" asked
Graham.

"This one—next to papa," she said, pointing to the door that led into the passage.

"Yes, you can stay there if you like; but don't you think you would be better with Madame Lavaux, than all by yourself in there?"

"No, I would rather stay here," she answered, and then pausing a moment at the door, "I may come and see him presently?" she added wistfully, "I always nursed him when he was ill before."

"I am sure you are a very good little nurse," said Graham kindly, "and I will tell you when you may come; but it will not be just yet. So the best thing you can do will be to go to bed, and then you will be quite ready for to-morrow."

He had no time to say more, for his services were required. He gave Madelon a candle, closed the door that communicated between the two rooms, and she was left alone.

CHAPTER II.

A FAREWELL LETTER.

MADELON was left alone to feel giddy, helpless, bewildered in the reaction from strong excitement and passion. She was quite tired and worn-out, too, with her long watching and waiting; too weary to cry even, or to think over all that had happened.

She did not go to bed, however; that would have been the last thing she would have thought of doing; for, Graham's last words notwithstanding, she had a notion that in a few minutes she would be called to

R 2

come and watch by her father, as she had often done in the old days at Florence; so she only put down her candle on the table, and curled herself up in a big arm-chair; and in five minutes, in spite of her resolution to keep wide awake till she should be summoned, she was sound asleep.

Low voices were consulting together in the next room, people coming in and out; the French doctor who had been sent for arriving; cautious footsteps, and soft movements about the injured man. But Madelon heard none of them, she slept soundly on, and only awoke at last to see her candle go out with a splutter, and the grey light of dawn creeping chilly into the room. She awoke with a start and shiver of cold, and sat up wondering to find herself there; then a rush of recollections came over her of last night, of her father's accident, and she jumped up quickly, straightening herself, stretching her little stiff limbs, and pushing back her tumbled hair with both hands from the sleepy eyes that were hardly fairly open even now.

Her first movement was towards the door between the two bedrooms, but she checked herself, remembering that Monsieur le Docteur had told her she must not go in there till she was called. There was another door to her room leading into the corridor, and just at that moment she heard two people stop outside it, talking together in subdued tones.

" Then I leave the case altogether in your hands," says a strange man's voice. " I am absolutely obliged to leave Paris for B—— by the first train this morning, and cannot be back till to-morrow night; so, as you say, Monsieur, you are in Paris for some time——"

" For the next few days, at any rate," answered the other; and Madelon recognized

Graham's voice and English accent, " long enough to see this case through to the end, I am afraid."

" If anything can be done, you will do it, I am sure,"interrupted the other with warmth. " You must permit me to say, Monsieur, as an old man may say to a young *confrère*, that it is seldom one meets with so much coolness and skill in such a very critical case. Nothing else could have saved——"

The voices died away as the speakers walked towards the end of the passage. Madelon had hardly taken in the sense of the few sentences she had heard; she was only anxious now to see Graham and ask if she might go to her father, so she opened her door softly and crept into the passage, meeting Horace as he returned towards the sick-room after seeing the French doctor off. He looked down on the little figure all pale and ruffled in the cold grey light.

"Why, I thought you were asleep," he said. "Would you like to see your father now? You may come in, but you must be very quiet, for he is dozing."

"Then he is better?" said Madelon, anxi- ously.

Graham did not answer; he opened the door and led her in. The room looked cheerless with the shaded night-lamp casting long shadows, which mingled with those that the growing daylight was chasing away. M. Linders was lying with his head support- ed on a heap of pillows; his forehead was bandaged where the deep cut had been given just above the brow, and he looked deadly pale; his eyes were closed, he was breathing heavily, and Madelon thought that, as Graham had told her, he was asleep ; but it was, in fact, rather a kind of stupor, from which louder noises than the sound of her soft footfall would have failed to rouse him.

She went on tiptoe up to his bedside, and stood gazing at him for a moment, and then with a swift, silent movement buried her face in her hands, and burst into an agony of crying.

" He is very ill—oh ! is he going to die ?" was all the answer she could give in a hoarse whisper to Graham's attempts at comfort, trying the while to smother her sobs, so that they might not break out and wake her father.

" I hope not—I hope not," said Horace, quite grieved at the sight of her distress ; "but you must not cry so, Madelon ; how are you to nurse him and help him to get well again if you do ?"

She stopped sobbing a little at this, and tried to check her tears.

" Do you really think he will get well again ?" she said ; " he looks so ill."

Graham did not at once answer.   In

truth, he saw no prospect of M. Linders' ultimate recovery, though he would probably regain consciousness, and might, perhaps, linger on for a few days. But there always remained the hope born of a determination not to despair, and it seemed cruel, at that moment, not to share it with our poor little Madelon.

"We must hope so," he said at last, "we must always hope for the best, you know; but he must be kept very quiet, so you and I, Madelon, must do our best to watch him, and see that he is not disturbed."

"Yes," said Madelon, drying her eyes quite now. "I will take care of him."

"Very well, then, if you will sit with him now, I will go and speak to Madame Lavaux, if she is up; there are several arrangements I have to make."

He went away, leaving Madelon contented for the moment, since she could sit and watch by her father; she remained motionless, her eyes fixed on his face, her hands clasped round her knees, her whole mind so absorbed in keeping perfectly quiet, the one thing she could do for him just then, that she hardly ventured to breathe. But not even yet did she understand the full meaning of what had happened, nor clearly comprehend all that she had to dread. She was not really afraid that her father would not recover; she knew indeed that he was very ill, much worse than he had ever been at Florence, and that it might be a long, long time before he would be well again, but she did not think that he was going to die. She had asked the question indeed, prompted by an instinctive terror that had seized her, but in fact she hardly knew what death meant, much less had she ever conceived of her father as dead, or imagined life without him. Nevertheless,

the sudden panic had left a nameless, un-
recognized fear lurking somewhere, which
gave an added intensity to her desire that
he would wake up and speak to her once
more; and sometimes the beating of her own
heart seemed to deafen her, so that she
could not hear the sound of his heavy ir-
regular breathing, and then nothing but the
dread of disturbing him could have pre-
vented her from jumping up and going to
him to make sure that he was still sleeping.
When would he awaken and look at her
and speak to her again? It appeared so
long since she had heard his voice, and seen
him smile at her; since he had wished her
good-bye the evening before, she seemed to
have lived through such long hours of unimagined terror and sorrow, and all without being able to turn to him for the sure
help, for the loving protection and sympathy that had ever been ready for his little

Madelon; and even now, he did not know how she was watching him, nor how she was longing to go to him and kiss him, to put her arms round his neck, and lay her soft little cheek caressingly against his. This thought was the most grievous of all to Madelon just then, and the big tears came into her eyes again, and fell slowly one by one into her lap.

Graham, however, returning presently, somehow seemed to bring courage and consolation with him. Madelon brightened up at once when he sat down by her and told her that he had asked Madame Lavaux to send them up some coffee, so that they might have it together there; and then, seeing the tears on her sad little face, he assured her in his kind way that her father would wake up presently and speak to her, and that, in the meantime, she need not sit quite so still, as she would not disturb him if she moved about quietly; and when, by-and-by, the *café-au-lait* arrived, they had their little meal together, whilst he told her in a low voice how her father had partially recovered his consciousness in the night and asked for her, but had been quite satisfied when he heard she had gone to bed, and had afterwards gone off to sleep as Madelon saw him now.

" By-the-by, Madelon," Graham said presently, " tell me if you have any relations living in Paris, or any friends that you go and visit sometimes ?"

" No," says Madelon wondering, " I have no relations—only papa."

" No uncles, or aunts, or cousins ?"

" No," said Madelon again, " only Uncle Charles, who died, you know."

" Ah, yes—that was an English uncle; but your papa, has he no brothers or sisters in Paris, or anywhere else ?"

"I never heard of any," said Madelon, to whom this idea of possible relations seemed quite a new one. "I never go to visit anyone."

"Then you have no friends living in Paris —no little companions, no ladies who come to see you?"

"No," answers Madelon, shaking her head, "we don't know anyone in Paris, except some gentlemen who come to play with papa—like Monsieur Legros, you know —only some are nicer than he is; but I don't know the names of them all. At Wiesbaden I knew a Russian princess, who used to ask me to go and see her at the hotel—oh, yes, and a German Countess, and a great many people that we met at the tables and at the balls, but I daresay I shall never see them again; we meet so many people, you know."

"And you have no other friends?"

"Oh, yes," said Madelon, her eyes shining suddenly, "there was the American artist, who lived in our house in Florence, and the old German who taught me to sing and play the violin; I was very fond of him, he was so good—so good."

"Who were they?" asked Graham.

Madelon explained, not in the least understanding the purport of all these questions, but her explanation did not help Graham much. In truth, he was revolving some anxious thoughts. In accepting the charge of this sick man, he felt that he had incurred a certain responsibility, not only towards M. Linders, but towards his little girl, and any relations or friends that he might have. It was on Madelon's account above all that he felt uneasy; what was to become of her if her father died—and Graham had little doubt that he was dying—all friendless and alone in the world as she

would apparently be? Had any arrangements for the future been made, any pro-
vision left for her? What was to become
of this poor child, clinging so closely to
her father, and so dependent upon him
that she seemed to have no thoughts nor
ideas apart from him?

Graham had been questioning Madame Lavaux as to what she knew of M. Linders and
his life, and had gained much information
on some points, though very little on others.
Madame Lavaux had readily related the
history of Madelon's birth and Madame
Linders' death. It was a story she was
fond of telling; it had been a little romance
in the ordinary routine of hotel life, and one
in which, when she had duly set forth M.
Linders' heartlessness and her own exertions, she felt that she must shine in an ex-
ceptionally favourable light; and indeed it
was so pitiful a tale that her hearers could

not but share the indignation and compassion she felt and expressed when she spoke of *cette pauvre dame*, who so young and so beautiful had been left alone to give birth to her infant, and, still alone, to die four months later. But when Graham endeavoured to get at any facts bearing directly upon the present emergency, he found Madame Lavaux less well-informed. M. Linders had come to her hotel year after year, she said, and she had always taken him in, on the little girl's account (who was a *chère petite*, though troublesome sometimes, as children would be); otherwise she would have been sorry to have such a *maurais sujet* about the house, in and out at all hours, and queer-looking men sitting up with him half the night. Had he any relations or friends? That she did not know, she had never seen or heard of any, but she did not wonder at that—they did well to keep clear of him, a bad man, who had broken more hearts than his wife's, she would answer for it. For the rest, she knew little about him, she added, with a sudden fit of professional reticence, induced by the recollection that it might be as well not to gossip too much about the affairs of her *clientèle*; he came and went, paid his bill regularly enough, generally seemed to have money at his command, and of course it was not for her to inquire how he got it, though she might have her suspicions. What was to become of his little girl in case of his death? Madame had never thought of that; did Monsieur think he was going to die? In that case how much better to have taken him to the hospital; a death in the house was always so inconvenient and disagreeable—not that she had grudged it to that *pauvre* Madame Linders, but this was a different thing altogether; would he certainly die? Monsieur said he did not know, one must always hope, but the case was a grave one, and seeing that Madame could give him no help he left her.

He had questioned Madeleine in the hope that she would be able to tell him of some one for whom he could send, or to whom he could at least write, but here again he was baffled, and he could only wait now for the moment when M. Linders should recover consciousness.

The hotel was all astir by this time with life and movement, doors opening and shutting, footsteps up and down the staircases and corridors, voices talking, calling, grumbling, downstairs eating and drinking going on with much clattering of plates and dishes, fiacres and omnibuses driving up, tourists setting off in gay parties for their day's sight-seeing, luggage being moved, travellers coming, travellers going, to Eng-

land, to the north, to the south, to the ends
of the earth—all the busy restless hotel life
going on except in this one silent room,
where two people sat very quietly watching
a third, who, as one of them foresaw sadly
enough, would never take part in all this
stir and bustle of life again. Outside was
broad sunny daylight now, but within it
was all dim and cool, for the night had been
hot, and the window stood wide open, and
now the morning air blew freshly through
the Venetian shutters, that were closed to
darken the room and shut out the sun,
which later would shine full upon them.
The morning hours slipped away; there was
nothing to be done while M. Linders remained in this state, and Madelon, by
Horace's advice, took a book, and seated
herself on a low stool by the window to
read. Now and then she would stand
looking at her father with a most pitiful

yearning in her great brown eyes; once or twice, M. Linders, in his dull slumber, half torpor, half sleep, seemed in some sort conscious of her presence; he moved his head uneasily, said "Madeleine," and then some low muttered words which she could not catch, but he never quite roused up, and after each throb of expectation and hope, she could only return to her book, and her silent watching.

Graham went in and out, or sat reading and writing at the table, and at twelve o'clock he made Madelon go downstairs to breakfast with Madame Lavaux in her own little sitting-room. Madame, who was really very fond of her, had forgotten all about the altercation of the night before. Indeed she was both good-natured and kind-hearted as soon as she could allow her better impulses to have their own way; but she was a little apt, as are most people to whom life

resolves itself into a narrow ministering to
their personal pains and pleasures, to look
upon untoward occurrences as evidence of
the causeless animosity of some vague im-
personality, continually on the watch to ad-
just the largest events of life so as to occasion her particular inconvenience. If half
Paris and its environs had been destroyed
by an earthquake, her first impression of the
catastrophe would very possibly have been
that it could not have happened at a worse
moment for raising the price of early as-
paragus, though the further reflection that
the general want of accommodation would
justify her in doubling her hotel tariff, might
in some measure have restored her faith in
the fitness of things. After this, she would
have found time to be overwhelmed with
compassion for the sufferers. M. Linders'
accident, she found, had, as yet, been attended with no evil results, so far as she

was concerned; no one had been disturbed in the night, no one had left, so that, for the moment, it had been safely transferred to that region of abstract facts, which she could consider dispassionately, and judge by the light of her kindly impulses; and it was under the influence of these that she was now bent on petting and making much of Madelon, giving her cakes and confitures and all kinds of good things. On second thoughts she had rejected the idea that M. Linders was going to die; it would be so very troublsome and inconvenient, that she found it pleasanter to persuade herself that he would surely recover; and now, on the strength of this conviction, and with a kind wish to console Madelon, she became so encouraging, so certain he would be well again in a few weeks—in a few weeks did she say?—in a few days—with this clever English doctor, who, as she improvised for the occasion, everyone knew was one of the first doctors in London—with all this Madame so encouraged and cheered our Madelon, that she came up-stairs again at the end of an hour looking quite bright, and almost expecting to see some wonderful change for the better in her father. M. Linders, however, still lay as she had left him, and perhaps the sight of his pale bloodless face chilled her, for she crept silently to her corner, and took up her book again, without saying a word of her new hopes. Presently Graham, looking up from his writing, found that she had done the best thing possible under the circum-stances, for, with her book lying open upon her lap, and her head resting against the window-frame, she had fallen fast asleep. He went up to her, raised her gently in his arms, and carried her into her own room ; so perfectly sound asleep was she, that she hardly stirred, even when he laid her on her bed; and then, drawing the curtain round her, he left her to herself.

If this long morning had passed slowly and sadly for our sorrowful little Madelon, it had been a time of anxiety and uneasiness enough for Horace Graham also; who had never, I daresay, felt more nervous than during these quiet hours when M. Linders, partly from the effects of his accident, partly from the opiates that had been given him, lay unconscious. He was young in his profession, and though clever and skilled enough in the technical part, he had had little experience in what may be called the moral part of it, and he positively shrank from the moment when this man, of whose life and character he knew something, should wake up, and he should have to tell him that he was dying. It was so absolutely necessary, too, that he should know the

danger he was in; for if, as was too probable from his mode of life, his affairs
were in disorder, and his arrangements for
his child's future had still to be made, the
time that remained to him was in all human
probability but short. For the rest, Graham
felt in himself small capacity for preaching
or exhortation, and indeed from a profes-
fesional point of view, he dreaded a possible
outburst of excitement and remorse, as les-
sening his last chance of saving his patient's
life; and yet to him—young, full of energy,
and hope, and resolution, though no nearer
perfection and tried wisdom than any other
man with crude beliefs and enthusiasms and
untested powers for good or evil—to him
death still appeared one of the most awful
facts in life, and he could not think unmoved
of the task of announcing to such a man as
this, that his last chances were over, and

such life as one can live in this world was for him a thing of the past for ever now. Not a twelvemonth later, Graham had stood by so many dying men, had listened to so many dying speeches, had seen death met in so many forms, and with such strange variety of character, with indifference or calmness, or resignation, with wild triumph, or wilder remorse, that he looked back with a sort of wonder on his present inexperience and perplexity. Not the less, however, did he now sit framing a dozen speeches one after the other, dreading the effect of saying too much, and fearing to say too little, till, about an hour after Madelon had fallen asleep, M. Linders at length stirred, opened his eyes, and tried to move.

Graham was at his side instantly, and the sick man gazed up at him in silence for a moment.

"What has happened?" he said at last

in a feeble voice; "who are you? where is Madelon?"

"Madelon is in the next room asleep," answered Graham; "you met with an accident last night—I am an English doctor staying in the hotel—the French one had to leave—do you remember?"

He paused between each sentence, and M. Linders' eyes, which were fixed upon him as he spoke, gradually acquired an expression of intelligence as memory returned to him. He closed them again and turned away his head.

"Yes, I remember something about it," he said, "but—*que diable*—I cannot move a limb: am I much hurt?"

"A good deal," said Graham, helping him to raise himself a little. "You had better keep quiet, and take this," giving him a cordial, as M. Linders sank back exhausted.

"That is better," he said, after a few

minutes of struggling breathing. "So I am a good deal hurt? Am I—am I going to die by chance, M. le Docteur?"

He spoke in his old half-sarcastic, half-cynical way, but with a feeble, gasping voice, that made an effect of contrast, as of the tragic face espied behind the grinning mask. Somehow it touched Graham, burdened as he was with the consciousness of the death-warrant he had to pronounce, and he paused before answering. M. Linders noticed his hesitation.

"Bah!" he said, "speak, then; do you think I am afraid—a coward that fears to know the worst? I shall not be the first man that has died, nor, in all probability, the last. We ought to be used to it by this time, *nous autres!*"

"Perhaps it is always best to be prepared for the worst," says Graham, recovering himself at this address, and taking refuge at last in a conventional little speech. "And though we must always hope for the best, I do not think it right to conceal from you, Monsieur, that you are very much injured and shaken. If you have any arrangements to make, anyone you would wish to send for, or to see, I earnestly advise you to lose no time."

He watched M. Linders narrowly as he spoke, and saw a sudden gleam of fear or excitement light up his dull eyes for a moment, whilst his fingers clutched nervously at the sheet, but that was all the sign he made.

"So—I am going to die?" he said, after a pause. "Well—that is ended, then. Send for anyone? Whom should I send for?" he added, with some vehemence. "For your priests, I suppose, to come and light candles, and make prayers over me—is that what you are thinking of, by chance? I won't have one of them—you need not think it, do you hear?—not one."

"Pardon me," said Graham, "but it was not of priests I was thinking just then—indeed, it seems to me that, at these moments, a man can turn nowhere so safely as to his God—but there are others——"

He spoke quietly enough, but M. Linders interrunpted him with a fierce, hoarse whisper. "I can arrange my own affairs. I have no one to send to—no one I wish to see. Let me die in peace."

In spite of his assumed indifference, his whole soul was filled and shaken with a sudden dread terror; for the moment he had forgotten even his child. Graham saw it, but could not urge him further just then ; he only passed his arm under the pillow, so as to raise his head a little, and then said, with such professional cheerfulness as he could muster,

" *Allons*, Monsieur, you must have courage. Calm yourself; you are not going to die yet, and we must hope for the best. You may live to see many people yet."

M. Linders appeared scarcely to hear what he was saying; but in a few moments his face relaxed, and a new expression came into it, which seemed to soften the grey, ghastly look.

"My poor little girl!" he said, with a sort of groan—"my little Madelon!—to leave thee all alone, *pauvre petite!*"

" It was precisely of her that I wished to speak," said Graham. " I am afraid, in any case, you must look forward to a long illness, and, on her account, is there no friend, no relation you would wish to send for?"

"I have no friends—no relations," said M. Linders, impatiently. " A long illness? Bah! M. le Docteur, I know, and you know that I am going to die—to-day, to-morrow, who knows?—and she will be left alone. She has no one in the world but me, and she has been foolish enough to love me—my little one!"

He paused for a moment, and then went on, with a vehemence that struggled for utterance, with his hoarse feeble voice and failing breath.

" If this cursed accident had happened but one day sooner or later, I could have left her a fortune—but a superb fortune; only one day sooner—I had it two days ago—or to-morrow—I should have had my revenge last night of that *scélérat*—that devil—that Legros, and won back the money he cheated me of, he—he—of all men, a mere beginner, a smatterer—ah! if I had been the man I once was, it would have been a different account to settle——"

He lay back panting, but began again before Graham could speak.

"I only want time—give me a little time, and my little Madeleine shall have such a fortune as shall make her independent of every one; or stay, why not send for him now? I will give you his address—yes, now—now at once, before it is too late!"

"That is quite impossible, Monsieur," Graham answered with decision; "and if you agitate yourself in this way, I must refuse to listen to another word. You are doing all you can to lessen your chances of recovery."

"You do not play, Monsieur?" said M. Linders, struck with a new idea, and not in the least attending to what Graham was saying.

"Do you want to win my money?" said the young man, half smiling. "No, I do not play, nor, if I did, have I any money to lose. Leave all these notions alone, I entreat of you; calm yourself; you need not

trouble yourself to speak much, but just tell
me what your wishes are concerning your
little girl—in any case it is always best to
be prepared. Have you made any will?
Is there any one to whose care you would
wish to entrust her in the event of your
death?"

M. Linders had exhausted his strength and
his passion for the moment, and answered
quietly enough. No, he had made no will,
he said—of what use? Everything he had
was hers, of course—little enough too. as
matters stood. He owned he did not know
what was to become of her; he had made
no arrangements—he had never thought of
its coming to this, and then he had always
counted on leaving her a fortune. He had
sometimes thought of letting her be brought
up for the stage; that might be arranged now,
if he could see S——, the manager of the

Théâtre ———. Could he be sent for at once?

"Certainly, if you really wish it," answered Graham with some hesitation, and then added frankly, "I have no sort of right to offer an opinion, but will you not consider a moment before fixing on such a fate for your child? She is surely very young to be thrown amongst strangers, on such a doubtful career, especially without you at hand to protect her."

"It is true I shall not be there," said the father with a groan; "I had forgotten that. And I shall never see my little one grown up. Ah! what is to become of her?"

"Has she no relations?" said Graham, "in England for instance———"

"In England!" cried M. Linders fiercely, "what could make you fancy that?"

"I had understood that her mother was English—" began Graham.

" You are right, Monsieur; her mother was English, but she has no English relations, or, if she has, they are nothing to her, and she shall never know them. No," he said slowly, after a pause, " I suppose there is only one thing to be done, and yet I would almost rather she lay here dead by my side, that we might be buried together in one grave; it would perhaps be happier for her, poor little one! Ah, what a fate! but it must be—you are right, I cannot send her out alone and friendless into the world, she must go to her aunt."

" She has an aunt, then," said Graham, with some surprise.

" Yes, Monsieur, she has an aunt, my sister Thérèse, with whom I quarrelled five and twenty years ago, and whom I have cordially hated ever since; and if ever woman deserved to be hated, she does;" and indeed, though he had not mentioned his

sister's name for years, the very sound of it
seemed to revive the old enmity in all its
fresh bitterness. "She lives near Liége,"
he went on presently. "She is the Superior
of a convent there, having risen to that emi-
nence through her superior piety and mani-
fold good works, doubtless. *Mon Dieu!*"
he cried, with another of his sudden impotent
bursts of passion and tenderness, "that it
should have come to this, that I should
shut up my little one in a convent! And she
will be miserable—she will blame me, she
will think me cruel; but what can I do?
what can I do?"

"But it seems to me the best thing possible," said Graham, who, in truth, was not
a little relieved by this sudden and unexpected solution of all difficulties. "So
many children are educated in convents,
and are very happy there; she will be certainly well taught and cared for, and you

must trust to your sister for the future."

"Never!" he said, half raising himself on his elbow with a mighty effort. "Well taught!—yes, I know the sort of teaching she will get there; she will be taught to hate and despise me, and then they will make her a nun—they will try to do it, but that shall never be! I will make Madelon promise me that. My little one a nun!—I will not have it! Ah! I risk too much; she shall not go!"

He fell back on the pillow gasping, panting, almost sobbing, all pretence and semblance of cynicism and indifference gone in this miserable moment of weakness and despair. Was it for this, then, that he had taught his child to love him—that he had watched and guarded and cherished her— that he should place her now in the hands of his enemy, and that she should learn to hate his memory when he was dead? Ah!

he was dying, and from the grave there
would be no return—no hand could be
stretched out from thence to claim her—no
voice make itself heard to appeal to her old
love for him, to remind her of happy by-
gone days when she had believed in him,
and to bid her be faithful to him still.
Those others would be able to work their
will then, while he lay silent for evermore,
and his little one would too surely learn
what manner of father she had had, perhaps
—who knows?—learn to rejoice in the day
that had set her free from his influence.

Graham very likely understood something
of what was passing in M. Linders' mind,
revealed, as it had been, by those few
broken words, for he said in a kind voice,

"I think you may surely trust to your
child's love for you, M. Linders, for she
seems to have found all her happiness in it
hitherto, and it is so strong and true that I

do not think it will be easily shaken, nor can I fancy anyone will be cruel enough to attempt it." And then, seeing how little capable M. Linders seemed at that moment of judging wisely, he went on to urge the necessity of Madelon's being sent to her aunt as her natural guardian, representing the impossibility of leaving her without money or friends in the midst of strangers.

"There is a little money," said M. Linders, "a few thousand francs—I do not know how much exactly; you will find it in that desk. It would start her for the stage; she has talent—she would rise. S—— heard her sing once; if he were here now, we might arrange——"

He was rambling off in a low broken voice, hardly conscious, perhaps, of what he was saying. Graham once more interposed.

"No, no," he said, "you must not think

of it. Let her go to her aunt. Don't be uneasy about her getting there safely; I will take charge of her."

"You will?" said M. Linders, fixing his dim eyes on Graham, and with some resumption of his old manner. "Pardon, Monsieur, but who are you, that you take such an interest in my affairs?"

"Anyone must take an interest in your little girl," said Graham warmly, and in the kind, frank voice that somehow always carried with it the conviction of his sincerity and good faith, "and I am truly glad that the chance that brought me to this hotel has put it in my power to be of use to you and to her. For the rest, my name is Graham, and I am an army surgeon. I don't suppose you recollect the circumstance, Monsieur, but I very well remember meeting you at Chaudfontaine some years ago."

"No, I don't remember," said M. Linders

faintly, " but I think I may trust you. You will see that Madelon reaches Liége safely?"

" I will take her there myself," answered Graham. " Would you like to send any message to your sister?"

" I will write," said M. Linders, " or rather you shall write for me; but presently—I cannot talk any more now—it must do presently."

Indeed he was faint from exhaustion, and Graham could only do all that was possible to revive him, and then remain by his side till he should have recovered his strength a little; and as he sat there, silently watching, I daresay he preached a little sermon to himself, but in no unfriendly spirit to his patient, we may be sure. This, then, was what life might come to—this might be the end of all its glorious possibilities, of all its boundless hopes and aims. To this man, as to another, had the great problem been

presented, and he had solved it—thus; and
to Graham, in the fulness of his youth, and
strength, and energy, the solution seemed
stranger than the problem. To most of us,
perhaps, as years go on, life comes to be
represented by its failures rather than its
successes, by its regrets rather than its
hopes; enthusiasms die out, illusions vanish,
belief in the perfectibility of ourselves and
of others fades, as we learn to realize the
shortness of life, the waywardness of human
nature, the baffling power of circumstances,
too easily allowed; but in their place, a
humble faith in a more perfect and satisfy-
ing hereafter, which shall be the comple-
ment of our existence here, the fulfilment of
our unfinished efforts, our many shortcom-
ings, springs up, let us trust, to encourage
us to new strivings, to ever-fresh beginnings,
which shall perhaps be completed and bear
fruit in another world, perhaps be left on

earth to work into the grand economy of progress—not wholly useless in any case. But at four or five and twenty, in spite of some failures and disappointments, the treasure of existence to an honest, frank heart, still seems inexhaustible as it is inestimable. The contrast between the future Graham looked forward to, full of hopes and ambitions, and this past whose history he could guess at, and whose results he contemplated, forced itself upon him, and an immense compassion filled the young man's heart at the sight of this wasted life, of this wayward mind, lighted up with the sudden, passionate gleams of tenderness for his child, the one pure affection perhaps that survived to witness to what had been— a great compassion, an honest, wondering pity for this man who had thus recklessly squandered his share of the common birth-right. Ah! which of us, standing on safe shores, and seeing, as all must see at times, the sad wreck of some shattered life cast up by the troubled waves at our feet, does not ask himself, in no supercilious spirit, surely, but with an awe-struck humility, "Who or what hath made thee to differ?"

Perhaps, as M. Linders lay there, he also preached to himself a little sermon, after his own peculiar fashion, for when, at the end of half an hour, he once more aroused himself, all signs of agitation had disappeared, and it was with a perfect calmness that he continued the conversation. Graham could not but admire this composure in the man whom but just now he had seen shaken with passion and exhausted with conflicting emotions; whom indeed he had had to help, and judge for, and support in his hour of weakness and suffering; whilst now M. Linders had resumed his air of calm superiority as the man of the world, which seemed at once to repel and to forbid support and sympathy from the youth and inexperience at his side.

"You are right, Monsieur," he said, breaking the silence abruptly, and speaking in a clear, though feeble voice, "Madelon must go to her aunt. Did I understand you to say you would take charge of her to Liége?"

"I will certainly," said Graham; "if——"

"I am exceedingly indebted to you," said M. Linders, "but I am afraid such a journey may interfere with your own plans."

"Not in the least," replied Graham. "I am only travelling for amusement, and have no one to consult but myself."

"Ah—well, I shall not interfere with your amusement long; and in the meantime, believe me, I am sensible of your goodness. It may make matters easier if you take a letter from me to my sister. I am afraid I cannot write myself, but I could dictate—if it be not troubling you too much—there are a pen and ink somewhere there; and if you could give me anything—I still feel rather faint."

Graham rose, gave him another cordial, drew a small table to the bedside, and sat down to write. M. Linders considered for a moment, and then began to dictate.

"MA SŒUR,—We parted five and twenty years ago, with a mutual determination never to see each other again—a resolution which has been perfectly well kept, and which there is no danger of our breaking now, as I shall be in my grave before you read this letter; and you will have the further consolation of reflecting that, as we have never met again in this world, neither is there any probability of our doing so in another——"

"Pardon me," said Graham, laying down his pen, as M. Linders dictated these last words, "but you are about to recommend your child to your sister's care; of what use can it be to begin with words that can only embitter any ill-feeling there may have been between you?"

"But it is a great consolation I am offering her there," says M. Linders, in his feeble voice. "However, as you will—*recommençons*; but no more interruptions, Monsieur, for my strength is not inexhaustible."

"Ma Sœur,—It is now five and twenty years since we parted, with the determination never to see each other again. Whether we have done well to keep to this resolution or not, matters little now; we shall, at any rate, have no temptation in the future to break it, for I shall be in my grave before

you receive this letter. I am dying, a fact
which may possess some faint interest for
you even now—or may not—that is not to
the purpose either. It is not of myself that
I would speak, but of my child. I am sending
her to you, Thérèse, as to the only relative
she has in the world; look on her, if you
prefer it, as your mother's only grandchild;
we had a mother once who loved me, and
whom you professed to love—for her sake
be kind to Madelon. I am not rich, and
without money I cannot leave her amongst
strangers, otherwise I would have found
some other means of providing for her; at
the same time, I do not send her to you
absolutely penniless—she will take to you
the sum of three thousand francs, which will
provide her board for the next two or three
years, at any rate; I do not cast her on
your charity. I have two requests to make,
and if your religion teaches you to have any

regard for the wishes of a dying man, I trust you will hold them sacred as such. In the first place, I demand of you that you should not bring her up to be a nun; she has not, and never will have, the slightest vocation— is not that the right word?—for such a life. My wish is that she should be educated for the stage, but I do not absolutely desire it; circumstances must in some measure decide, and something must be left to your discretion, but a nun she shall not be. In the second place, respect my memory, so far as my little Madeleine is concerned. Keep your powers of abusing me, if they be not already exhausted, for the benefit of others; she has never been separated from me since she was an infant, and the little fool has actually learnt to love me, and to believe in me. It is an innocent delusion, and has made her happy—do not disturb it. I tell you, my sister, it will be the worst work you have

yet wrought upon earth, and an evil day for
you, if, even when I am in my grave, you try
to come between me and my daughter.

"Your brother,

"ADOLPHE LINDERS."

"I will sign it," said the sick man, holding out his hand for the pen. He had dictated the letter with some pauses and gasps
for breath, but in the uniform indifferent
voice that he had adopted since the beginning of the conversation. He dropped the
pen, when he had scrawled the signature
with almost powerless fingers, and his hand
fell heavily on the bed again. "That is
done," he said, and, after a pause, continued,
"Monsieur, circumstances have compelled
me to place a confidence in you, with which,
at another time, I should have hesitated to
burden you, fearing to cause you inconvenience."

"You cause me no inconvenience, and I shall do my best to carry out your wishes," said Horace. "In return, I must beg of you to keep yourself quiet now."

"One moment, Monsieur—my money you will find in that desk, as I have said; after paying my funeral and other expenses, you will, I think, find there is still the sum left that I have named in my letter. I must beg of you to hand it over to my sister. I can trust her so far, I believe; and I will not have my child a pauper on her hands, dependent on her charity for food and clothing; otherwise it might have been wiser—however, it is too late now, and in two or three years much may happen. One word more, and I have done. I have no sort of claim on your kindness, Monsieur, but you have proved yourself a friend, and as such I would ask you not to lose sight of Madelon entirely. She will be but a friendless little one when I am gone, and I have not much confidence in her aunt's tender mercies."

"You may depend upon it that I will not," said Graham earnestly, and hardly thinking of the sort of responsibility he was accepting.

"Thank you; then that is all. And now, Monsieur le Docteur, how long do you give me?"

"How long?" said Graham.

"Ah! how long to live?—to-day, to-night, to-morrow? How long, in short?"

Then Graham spoke plainly at last, without further reticence or concealment, so useless in the face of this indifference and levity, real or affected.

"M. Linders," he said, "the chance on which your recovery hangs is so slight, that I do not think it probable, hardly possible, that you can live over to-morrow. Will you not try to understand this?"

There was something so wistful and kind and honest in Graham's expression as he stood there, looking down on his patient, that M. Linders was touched, perhaps, for he held out his hand with a little friendly gesture; but even then he could not, or would not abandon his latest pose of dying *en philosophe.*

"I understand well enough," he answered; "a man does not arrive at my age, *mon ami,* without having faced death more than once. You think, perhaps, it has terrors for me?— not at all; to speak frankly, pain has, but I do not suffer so much now. That is a bad sign, perhaps. Well, never mind, you have done your best for me, I know, and I thank you. Except for that little regret that you know of as regards Legros and—and Madelon, I am content that life should come to an end—it is not too delightful in any case, and those that I cared for most did their best to spoil mine for me. For people who believe in a hereafter, and choose to contemplate a doubtful future, adorned with flames and largely peopled with devils, I can imagine death to have its unpleasant side; but I look upon all such notions as unphilosophical in the extreme. And now, Monsieur, I think I could sleep a little. By-and-by, when Madelon awakes, I should like to see her."

He turned his head away, and presently fell into a light dose. Did he mean, or did he persuade himself that he meant half of what he said? Graham could not decide; and, in truth, he had uttered his little speech with an air of dignity and resignation that half imposed upon the younger man, and impressed him, in spite of his better judgment. An heroic soul going forth with an

unfeigned stoicism to meet its fate? Or an
unhappy man, striving to hide a shivering
consciousness from himself, and others with
an assumption of philosophical scepticism?
Ah! who was Graham, that he should
judge or weigh the secrets of another man's
heart at such an hour as this? He left
the bedside, and went back once more to
his writing.

A few minutes afterwards, Madame Lavaux knocked softly, and looked into the
room. Graham went out into the passage
to speak to her, closing the door after him.

"How is he now, the poor Monsieur?"
asks Madame.

"He is sleeping now," Graham answered;
"there is nothing to be done but to keep
him as quiet as possible."

"And will he recover, do you think?"

"Hardly. One must always hope; but
he is very ill."

"Ah! well," said the landlady, resigning herself; "but, after all," she added, "it is sad to see a man die like that; and then there is the child. Otherwise the world will be none the worse for wanting him. But what is to become of the little girl?"

"That is all arranged," replied Graham, "she is to go to an aunt, a sister of her father's, who, it appears, is Superior of a convent near Liége. But can you tell me, Madame, had Madame Linders quarrelled with her English relations? When she was dying alone here, had she no friends of her own that she could have sent for to be with her?"

"She would not have them, Monsieur; you see, she was devoted to her husband in spite of all, this poor Madame, and *he* had quarrelled with her relations, I believe; at any rate, she would not send for them. 'Adolphe will come,' she would always say, 'and it would vex him to find anyone here,' and so she died alone, for he never arrived till the next morning. However," continues Madame, "it was not of that I came to speak now, it was to know if Monsieur would not wish to have a nurse to-night to attend to the poor gentleman? It is what we must have had if you had not been here, and there is no reason why you should knock yourself up with nursing him."

"It certainly might be better," said Graham considering, "I had thought of it, but —however, you are quite right, Madame, a nurse we will have; where can I get one?"

Madame said he had better apply to the Sœurs de Charité, and gave him an address, adding that if he would like to go himself she could spare half an hour to sit with Monsieur there.

"I will go at once," replied Graham, "whilst he is sleeping; he is not likely to rouse again just at present; don't let him talk or move if he should awake, but it is not probable that he will."

So it was arranged, and Madame Lavaux established herself with her knitting in the dim, silent room, whilst Graham departed on his errand, satisfied that his patient was in safe hands. Not ten minutes had elapsed, however, when a knock came at the door of the sick-room, and a summons —could Madame come at once? Madame cast a look at her charge; he was perfectly still and quiet, sleeping profoundly apparently; there could be no harm in leaving him for a moment. She went, intending to return immediately; but, alas! for human intentions, downstairs she found a commotion that drove M. Linders, M. le Docteur, and everything else out of her head for the time being. Madame la Comtesse *au premier* had lost her diamond ring—her ring, worth six thousand francs, an heirloom, an inestimable treasure; lost it? it had been stolen—she knew it, felt convinced of it; she had left it for five minutes on her dressing-table whilst she went to speak to some dressmaker or milliner, and on her return it had vanished. Unpardonable carelessness on her part, she admitted, but that did not alter the fact; it had been stolen, and must be found; house, servants, visitors, luggage, all must be searched and ransacked. Where were the gendarmes? let all these people be taken into custody at once, pointing to the group of startled, wondering, servants,—let everyone be taken into custody. Madame Lavaux had enough to do and to think of for the next hour, we may be sure, and though, at the end of that time, Madame la Comtesse found the ring safe in the corner of her pocket, whither it had slipped off her finger, and the disturbance was at an end, not so were the consequences of that disturbance.

For in the meantime a very different scene was being acted out upstairs.

END OF THE FIRST VOLUME.

LONDON: PRINTED BY MACDONALD AND TUGWELL, BLENHEIM HOUSE.